"I'm so happy to meet you," Chloe said.

"Yeah, you're the notebook girl," Zinnie said.

Marigold felt her brow furrow. What was Zinnie talking about?

"My sister has a wild imagination—" Marigold started, but Chloe didn't look surprised at all.

"Wait, you saw me writing in my notebook?" Chloe asked.

"Yes," Zinnie said. Zinnie pulled her own notebook out of her pocket. "I'm a notebook girl, too."

Marigold felt a sting of jealousy. When Marigold and Pilar were still best friends, she worried that Pilar liked Zinnie better than her. Was that going to happen with Chloe?

THE SILVER SISTERS STORIES
by Leila Howland
The Forget-Me-Not Summer
The Brightest Stars of Summer
The Silver Moon of Summer

the Silver Moon of Summer

LEILA HOWLAND

Illustrated by Ji-Hyuk Kim

HARPER

An Imprint of HarperCollinsPublishers

ISBN 978-0-06-231876-3

Typography by Kate J. Engbring
18 19 20 21 22   CG/BRR   10 9 8 7 6 5 4 3 2 1
❖
First paperback edition, 2018

For Giff and Maryhope, and Aunt Dot,

whom we loved so very much

1 · Dive In

"One . . . two . . ." Zinnie's toes were curled up on the edge of the lighthouse diving board. Her palms tingled with anticipation, and her heart was in her throat as Marigold, Lily, Aunt Sunny, and Tony all counted together. Zinnie gulped a breath of air and plugged her nose as they all said, "Three!"

"Woo-hoo!" Zinnie shouted, and jumped. The air skimmed her body. Then she plunged into the cold, salty water. As it engulfed her, she felt the possibility of all that was ahead in the next two and a half weeks.

The Silver sisters were back in Pruet, Massachusetts, for their third summer, and Zinnie was certain it was going to be the best yet. The town was celebrating its tricentennial—its three hundredth birthday—and there was going to be a ton of activities, like an epic sand castle building contest; a parade from Charlotte Point all the way to the town beach; a sailing race with Omgansett, the next town over; a clambake at the yacht club and a dance at the casino. This first dip into Buzzards Bay was just the beginning.

Zinnie flipped onto her back and gazed up at the clear blue sky. After their long plane ride from Los Angeles—during which Zinnie had read the entire third novel in the Dream Weavers series, Marigold had watched two and a half movies, and Lily had mostly slept—the cold water was refreshing. It was six p.m. here, but only seemed like three o'clock because they were still on West Coast time. She felt like she had the whole day in front of her to think and dream about what she would be writing for her blog.

As an eighth grader in the fall, Zinnie would have the chance to be the editor in chief of *Muses*, the school's literary magazine. During the first meeting of the school year, the members of Mrs. Lee's Writers' Workshop would nominate candidates, and at the next meeting they'd vote.

Zinnie loved being in the Writers' Workshop, and she really wanted to be the editor in chief. She'd noticed that it was mostly just the members of the Writers' Workshop who read *Muses*. Zinnie was hoping to create something that everyone wanted to read, and couldn't put down until they'd devoured the whole thing, like one of Aunt Sunny's surprise brownies.

Muses should live up to its name and inspire people. As editor in chief, Zinnie felt she could make that happen.

But first she was going to have to get nominated! And then, of course, she'd have to win. The blog that Mrs. Lee assigned each member of the Writers' Workshop to keep over the summer was Zinnie's opportunity to prove not only her talent for writing, but also for connecting with readers. She needed to think of what Mrs. Lee called a "hook," a clever way to get the audience's attention, and then she'd have to find a way to keep her readers hooked. "A hook with legs," Mrs. Lee had said during the last meeting before school let out.

Zinnie had brainstormed on the beach in Malibu, bouncing some ideas off her dad, before they left L.A. She'd also journaled about it, and of course, she'd been obsessing about it on the plane ride to Boston, even while she was reading her book.

So far nothing was coming to mind, but she was hopeful that was going to change soon. Pruet was where she found some of her best ideas. As she swam her way back to the lighthouse in the smooth, even strokes she'd been practicing all winter, the salt pleasantly stinging her skin, she was sure her mind was opening up.

"Is it freezing?" Marigold asked as she watched Zinnie climb the ladder up the side of the lighthouse to the porch.

"Invigorating," Zinnie said through chattering teeth.

"Was it scary?" Lily asked as Zinnie climbed onto the wooden porch, which was warm from a long day in the sun.

"More like thrilling," Zinnie said, patting her little sister on the head.

"You dripped on me!" Lily said. "It *is* cold."

Aunt Sunny stood nearby, holding open a striped beach towel. Zinnie left wet footprints as she ran into her aunt's toweled embrace.

"I'm so delighted you're back, my dear," Aunt said, squeezing Zinnie tight.

"Me too," Zinnie said. Something about Aunt Sunny's hugs was deeply reassuring and comforting. It was as though she could hold the whole world still for a moment with her arms. "There's nothing like summer in Pruet."

"Summer is our reward for getting through the tough winters," Tony said.

"Especially this winter," Aunt Sunny said as she rubbed Zinnie's back. "The storms were vicious."

Aunt Sunny had told them all about the blizzards that she and Tony had endured. There had been three in a row, knocking out the power for days. Tony and Aunt Sunny had had to sleep in the living room in front of the roaring fireplace to keep warm. Luckily, Aunt Sunny's house had withstood the high winds, but not everyone had been so fortunate. Some of the houses closer to the shore had to be rebuilt, and the roof of the yacht club had been seriously damaged.

But now the sun stretched their shadows, and birds sang back and forth above her sisters' voices. They were discussing who would jump off the diving board next.

"You go," Marigold said to Lily. "I need to be a little warmer."

"But you're bigger than I am," Lily said. "And it's so high!"

"Zinnie already said it wasn't too scary," Marigold said.

"There's no reason to bicker, loves. You don't have to jump today," Aunt Sunny said. The lines around her eyes seemed more deeply etched than usual.

"Is it true that the Pruet town council chooses one boy and one girl to lead the parade at the tricentennial?" Zinnie asked, trying to distract her sisters. Zinnie didn't like to see Aunt Sunny looking worried, so she changed the subject to something she'd read about in the *Buzzards Bay Bugle*.

"That's right," Tony said. "The town council will nominate a young man and young woman who embody the spirit of James and Eliza Pruet, the town's founding family."

"Wait, what?" Marigold asked.

Zinnie's tactic had worked—her sisters had stopped fighting.

"They were said to be hardworking, spirited, and of course, very civic-minded. And the town council thought it would be fun to pick two people who embodied these same qualities to lead the parade on horseback," Aunt Sunny said.

"Horses? Wow. What does 'civic-minded' mean?" Lily asked.

"It means that you care about the community," Marigold answered. "Do they have to dress up in an old-fashioned way or get to wear anything . . . special?"

"There won't be any costumes, if that's what you mean. But Jean has offered to make a floral wreath for our Eliza and a matching corsage for James," Aunt Sunny said. "She's been taking a lot of courses on flower arranging this year. She says it's the new yoga."

"Cool," said Marigold with a dreamy look in her eyes. Zinnie felt pretty certain Marigold was imagining that she and Peter Pasque would be picked to be Eliza and James.

"I didn't know about the horseback part," Zinnie said with a smile. She didn't care about wearing a floral wreath on her head, but she did think it would be fun to ride on a horse next to Max down the main street. Max was Tony's grandson and Zinnie's first boy-who-was-a-friend, though Zinnie had sometimes wondered if he might be her boyfriend. Now, she looked down at her arms and noticed she had goose bumps. Was it the breeze that had given them to her or the idea of seeing Max again soon?

"So, Tony, when is Max coming?" Zinnie asked.

"I think they arrive a few days before the tricentennial," Tony replied.

"That'll be fun," Zinnie said, though she felt disappointed. She and Max messaged back and forth sometimes, so she knew that he was going to be living in Italy for a while. The last time she'd heard from Max, he wasn't sure how long their summer visit to Pruet was going to be. It all depended on his dad's time off from the military. As the sting of disappointment sharpened, she realized how much she'd been hoping he'd be here the whole time she was, not just for a few days.

"You really want to see Max, huh?" Marigold asked in a teasing voice.

"So, are you going to jump or not?" Zinnie asked, embarrassed that Marigold had seen through her so easily.

"There'll be plenty of time for swimming," Aunt Sunny said. "But now I think we should get you girls settled in."

"This year I'd like the bed near the window," Lily said.

"Hey, that's always been my bed!" Marigold said.

"Just because you're the oldest doesn't mean you always get what you want," Lily said.

Zinnie realized that she wanted that bed as well—the view might inspire her. She was about to put in her two cents, but decided against it.

The sisters had plenty of arguments at home, but for some reason their worst fights happened here in Pruet. Maybe this was because their parents weren't around to stop them. Or perhaps it was because they were all sharing a room. Or possibly it was because summer, with its freewheeling days and long twilights, simply had more room for everything—happiness, dreams, ideas, and even conflict. Their first summer here, Lily had almost drowned because Zinnie and Marigold had been fighting. And then last summer, they'd ruined Aunt Sunny's wedding cake because of another big argument. The idea of fighting again this year made her feel seasick. And the crease in Aunt Sunny's brow was getting deeper by the second.

"Hey, guys, can we make a deal?" Zinnie asked.

"Depends what it is," Marigold said.

"Come here," Zinnie said, and motioned for her sisters to join her in a huddle on the far end of the porch.

"Let's not fight this summer in Pruet. Let's promise to get through the two weeks in peace," Zinnie said. "For Aunt Sunny."

"Fine with me," Lily said. "But can you two really handle it?"

"Of course we can," Marigold said, visibly annoyed that her younger sister was questioning her.

"Shake on it?" Zinnie asked, extending a hand. Marigold took her sister's hand in her own. Lily used both hands to cover her sisters', and the three of them shook.

"So then," Lily asked. "Who gets the bed?"

2 · Three Wishes

"I can't sleep," Marigold said into the darkness of their attic bedroom. With its three narrow beds, one shared bureau, and the dollhouse that had been Aunt Sunny's when she was a girl, the room was exactly the same as she remembered it. "Anyone awake?"

Marigold held her breath and listened, but no one replied. She tucked her hair behind her ears, sat up, and gazed out the window—which was right next to her bed. Marigold had won the number guessing game they'd devised to see which sister would get the best bed. And as she pulled back the curtains to get a better view, she was satisfied she'd prevailed.

The sky was a dazzling array of stars. It seemed to be practically begging her to make a wish. She located the North Star, which was easy because it was one of the brightest, and thought for a moment. Then she said to herself, *I wish to find a perfect friend in my new school*. She had been thinking about transferring schools ever since the clique of mean girls in her class had started excluding her in seventh grade, and after another year of it in eighth, she'd finally decided to switch schools.

The event that really put her over the edge was when her former best friend, Pilar, officially ditched her for the Cuties clique last September by not inviting Marigold to her fourteenth birthday party, which was a sleepaway weekend in Big Bear Lake, in a nearby mountain town. When she asked Pilar about it later, she'd told Marigold that she thought she wouldn't have fun because she wasn't in the clique. Marigold not only felt like she'd been punched in the gut, she'd also lost some respect for her old friend.

For her own fourteenth birthday, which had been in the spring, her mom had taken her and her sisters out for a fancy tea at a hotel in Beverly Hills. It had always been her mom's rule that Marigold either invite the whole class or only her best friend. Since she didn't have a best friend anymore, and she didn't want the whole class to come, she decided to just celebrate with her family. They all got dressed up, and Zinnie spoke in a British accent the whole time. It was fun, but it didn't feel much like a birthday.

That was when Marigold announced to her mom that she really wanted to make a switch for high school. To her surprise, her mom agreed with her on the spot.

Marigold was thrilled when she got into the prestigious Performing Arts Magnet school, also known as PAM, where she was going to be able to focus on all her favorite things: acting, design, costumes, and even directing. She was looking forward to all the other artists she was going to meet at PAM. She knew that artists weren't like the Cuties. Everything was going to be better there. The school was across town, close to the beach, but her parents were willing to drive her.

As hopeful as Marigold was about her friend wish coming true, and as happy as Marigold was about her acceptance to PAM, she was also sad she was *really* losing Pilar now. Different schools were like different universes. They'd probably never see each other again.

Suddenly, here in her bed at Aunt Sunny's, she was anxious. She'd gone to school at Miss Hadley's since kindergarten. She would be starting school with absolutely no one she knew, traveling to a campus that was completely unfamiliar and three times the size of her old school. And she'd be going to school with boys for the first time since preschool! Boys! Marigold's heart pounded. She took several deep breaths. Boys weren't so bad, she told herself. Actually, she really liked boys, or at least one boy: Peter Pasque.

Oh, Peter Pasque! Her heart fluttered faster at the thought of him! It was amazing how quickly anxiety could transform into delightful nervousness. She smiled, picturing him on his sailboat. When would she get to see him? Tomorrow, she hoped. Yes—she would go to find him at the yacht club after sailing practice, which she knew ended around two thirty in the afternoon. She'd taken some sailing lessons in Redondo Beach over the school year. It would be so much fun to surprise him with her sailing skills this summer. And it would happen soon. Tomorrow was not so far away at all. At least, not if she could get to sleep. And then of course there was the dance during the tricentennial. Would she and Peter be chosen to be Eliza and James Pruet? It would be so dreamy to ride on a horse next to him, especially with a wreath of flowers in her hair! Would she even be eligible to be Eliza if she was merely a summer visitor?

She and Peter had kept in touch during the year, emailing and chatting online once or twice a month, especially when certain constellations were in the sky—they had a thing about the stars. Their families sent each other cards over the holidays, and Marigold had placed the one from the Pasques, which had a picture of Peter in a fisherman's sweater, in a special box of private things. For some reason she had trouble picturing him in anything but that fisherman's sweater now.

Could she make two wishes tonight? She didn't see why not. After all, there were plenty of stars in the sky. She needed to find another good star to wish to see Peter as soon as possible! Oh, and she also wanted to wish that he didn't have a girlfriend already. Make that three stars. She pressed her face against the screen and searched for the two next brightest stars. Thinking she'd have a better selection if she could lean out a little farther, she unfastened the clips that held the screen in place and gently put the screen on the floor.

Feeling as romantic as Juliet on her balcony, she leaned out the window to look around. In the story, Juliet was fourteen too, Marigold remembered. The air was still and warm and smelled green and fresh, just like country air should. An idea occurred to her—a wonderful, summery idea. Maybe she and Peter could be like Romeo and Juliet this summer. And he could secretly visit her outside this window late at night! She took a deep breath, imagining the sight of Peter calling up to her from below. Just as she leaned out a little more, something small and dark and fast as a bullet whooshed by her ear.

"Ahh!" she shrieked as she watched the dark form dart around the room. "Aaaaaahhh!"

3 · A Shadow in the Rafters

"What happened?" Zinnie asked, sitting up. It was dark and she was totally disoriented, but her sister's screams woke her up immediately. "Marigold, are you okay?"

"It's alive! It's in the rafters!" Marigold said, her voice spiking with fear.

"Huh?" Zinnie asked, trying to make sense of the situation. "Where are you?"

"Down here!" Marigold said. "Under the bed." That's when Zinnie saw that Marigold was on the floor, covering her hair. "Don't be an idiot, Zinnie. Duck! Or it'll get you!"

"What will?" Zinnie asked, dropping to the floor with some annoyance. She didn't appreciate being called an idiot.

"That!" Marigold said, pointing up.

"Eek!" Zinnie screamed when she saw the shadowy animal in the rafters. It had beady little eyes and wings.

"That thing!" Marigold said. *Whoosh!* It buzzed as it flew past Zinnie and swooped back up to the ceiling.

"AHH!" Zinnie said, diving under the bed. "A bat!"

"Be careful—it might get into your hair and build a nest!" Marigold said, her eyes as wide as Mochi ice cream balls. "And I don't know how it'd ever get out. You'd probably have to shave your head!"

"What?" Zinnie said, and covered her hair.

"Stop it, you two!" Lily said in a firm but calm voice. "You're scaring it. It's just a little old bat."

"That might have rabies," Marigold whimpered, grabbing her covers from the bed and wrapping herself like a mummy.

"Oh no!" Zinnie said, copying her sister and yanking a sheet around her head like a Russian babushka. "Rabies!"

"Hardly any bats have rabies," Lily said in a measured voice, and she tilted her head to the ceiling. "Hush now, bat. Don't you worry. I'm going to get you out of here safely."

"Lily—just get Aunt Sunny," Zinnie said as she scurried across the floor to join Marigold under her bed. Zinnie had taken a wilderness survival class this year at school. It had been a three-day trip in the Angeles

National Forest with the school camping club. Now, she could start a fire using flint, and pitch a leakproof tent. She even knew how to hang food in a tree to keep it away from bears. But bats? In the house? That was something else entirely. She watched as Lily tiptoed over to the bedroom door and closed it.

"Lily!" Marigold said, now clearly on the verge of tears. "What are you trying to do? Get us all bitten? Do you want us to get rabies?"

"In case you don't remember, I did my science fair project on bats!" Lily replied. "And I won!"

"We know," Zinnie said as she and Marigold clung to each other. "But this isn't science fair, this is real life. Please get Aunt Sunny!"

"Bats don't bite unless they feel incredibly threatened. They're actually delicate creatures who are important to the life cycle," Lily said. Marigold grunted in frustration. "And they're threatened in many parts of the world."

"I don't care," Marigold whined. "I just want him out without infecting any of us!"

"You should care," Lily said as she began to remove her pillow from its case. "Do you have any idea what would happen to the planet without bats? And this little guy is probably feeling so alone. Bats hardly ever travel alone. Aw, poor little bat. He's actually kind of cute."

"You absolutely cannot keep him," Zinnie said. Lily was crazy about animals—all animals, but especially those she studied.

"Aunt Sunny!" Marigold called.

"Lily, get down!" Zinnie said as she watched her sister climb onto her bed and approach the bat. "That is a wild animal," Zinnie continued, trying to appeal to her little sister's rational side. "It's not used to humans, and what you're doing is dangerous."

At that very moment the bat emitted a high-pitched squeak that caused Marigold to squeeze Zinnie so tightly, she thought she was going to pass out. Marigold wasn't much of a hugger, so it was always a bit of a surprise when Marigold turned to her for help, which she did during scary movies. As Zinnie wrapped her arm around her sister, she could smell her expensive shampoo, which Marigold didn't like to share since she saved her allowance for it.

"Echolocation!" Lily said with delight. "I think he's calling his friends."

"No!" Zinnie and Marigold both screamed. At that moment Lily leaped toward the bat, covered it with the pillowcase, and guided it to the open window, where she set it free and shut the window tight behind it. Zinnie exhaled with relief.

Marigold was taking shallow, nervous breaths as Aunt Sunny and Tony entered the room in their bathrobes and slippers. In spite of the current drama, Zinnie couldn't help but think it was cute that their silhouettes matched.

"What's going on?" Aunt Sunny asked, flipping on the lights.

"There was a bat!" Zinnie said. Marigold was still gripping her arm.

"In here?" Tony asked. "In the house?"

"Don't worry, Aunt Sunny. I safety brought him outside," Lily said. "Using only my scientific knowledge and this pillowcase."

"Good gracious!" Aunt Sunny exclaimed. Zinnie wasn't sure she'd ever seen Aunt Sunny so genuinely alarmed. "Are you okay? Did you get bit?"

"No!" Lily said. "It was a sweet bat. Just a baby, I think."

"For heaven's sake," Aunt Sunny said, pulling Lily toward her and examining her skin for any marks. "You're sure it didn't bite you?"

"Of course I'm sure," Lily said. "I think I'd know if it did."

"You have a point there," Aunt Sunny said, embracing Lily and kissing the top of her head.

Zinnie had a flash of her sister turning into some kind of bat vampire. That would definitely make a good blog! Would a fiction blog work? she wondered. "Sister gets bitten by a bat" was a great hook, and if she slowly transformed into a vampire, that would give the blog legs.

"I didn't make any contact except with the pillowcase," Lily said. "And I don't see any droppings, so that's a good thing. Bat poop can carry disease."

"You really should have come to get me and Tony," Aunt Sunny said to Lily. "It's not okay to handle a bat. But I have to admit, I'm impressed."

"They're such intelligent creatures. I knew that the bat trusted me," Lily said. "I also think he knew that these two were his enemies."

Lily pointed to her sisters. Zinnie and Marigold shook their heads, but honestly, they had been pretty panicked. Lily was the only one who'd kept her cool. *How is a seven-year-old not scared of bats?* Zinnie wondered, remembering that two summers ago, Lily was petrified of swimming in the ocean. Yet here she was, capturing creatures in pillowcases.

"I'm pretty dang certain I'd know if we had an infestation," Tony said, checking the rafters and the corners of the room.

"It was a lone bat. I'm, like, almost a hundred percent sure," Lily said, sounding like an adult. She sighed. "Well, I guess I'd better go wash my hands."

"I'll say," Aunt Sunny said. "With hot water and plenty of soap, and please give me that pillowcase."

Lily handed the pillowcase to Aunt Sunny, who held it pinched between her thumb and forefinger.

"Are we going to . . . use that again?" Zinnie asked, pointing at the pillowcase. Marigold was making a face like she'd eaten a lemon.

"I think not," Aunt Sunny said.

"I guess this is how it got in," Tony said, walking across the room and picking up the screen. "Not much of a mystery here."

"How'd that come off?" Aunt Sunny asked.

"Yeah," Zinnie wondered aloud. "How did it?"

"I took it off," Marigold confessed. "I was . . . looking around."

"Why?" Zinnie asked. There was a story here. She could feel it.

"I couldn't sleep," Marigold said defensively. "And I was hot."

"Huh," Aunt Sunny said as she put the screen back in place and fastened it.

"Huh," echoed Zinnie.

"Lily's right. There aren't any droppings," Tony said. "I'll give this house a once-over tomorrow morning, but I'm almost certain it was one bat. Just flew in by mistake."

After Aunt Sunny and Tony had gone back to bed, and Lily had settled back down with her fresh pillowcase, Zinnie asked, "Uh, Marigold, why did you take the screen off? Were you planning on running away or something?"

"I was just getting fresh air," Marigold said. "I told you. I couldn't sleep."

"She was probably looking for Peter," Lily chimed in.

"*Ohhhhh,*" Zinnie said. "Were you?"

Marigold was silent for a moment.

"Well?" Lily asked. "Am I right?"

"I was looking at the stars," Marigold said. "Good night."

"Interesting," Zinnie said. "Were you going to climb out and find him?"

"No!" Marigold said. "That's all I'm going to say on this subject. Now good night, good night, good night!"

"Good night," Zinnie said. "Don't let the bedbugs bite! Or the bats!"

Lily giggled, and Zinnie drifted off into her own thoughts. There was definitely some intrigue in this Marigold situation, but of course, Zinnie didn't dare write anything about her sister. Not after last summer when she'd read Marigold's diary and gotten into such trouble, not to mention losing her very own sister's trust for what felt like forever. Marigold still brought it up every now and then. But bats, on the other hand, were fair game.

4 · The Elusive Idea

Early the next morning, while her sisters were still sleeping, Zinnie brought her laptop to the corner of the yard where there was a Wi-Fi signal. Last summer Zinnie had used Aunt Sunny's office, which had been cleaned out for Tony, as her own private writing room. It'd had a little desk and almost nothing else in it, and Zinnie had relished the privacy it gave her. This summer that room was Tony's office, and it was full of building plans, tools, and all of his guitar stuff, so Zinnie had decided that the picnic table in the backyard, which Tony had built especially in anticipation of the girls' visit, was her new writing space. It was under the big beech tree and was the very place where Zinnie had first had the idea to write her first play two summers ago.

It was a shady spot, and the sunshine through the

leaves created a dappled effect. Even though there wasn't a door to close like there was in her office, it was far enough from the house that she couldn't get distracted by her sisters, but close enough to the back door that a snack was never very far away. She just needed to remember to make sure her laptop was totally charged in advance.

After checking to see if she had an email from Max—she didn't, bummer—she went right to the Miss Hadley's School for Girls Writers' Workshop website, which had the links to her fellow writers' blogs. All the girls in the group had set up their blogs using templates before the last day of school. As Zinnie clicked on each link, she saw that she was the only one who hadn't personalized her blog yet. The other girls obviously all had their ideas, and some of them even had their first two posts. The assignment was to write two posts a week for eight weeks. It was almost the end of the first week, and she was already behind!

The competition for editor in chief of *Muses* was stiff. Zinnie wanted it so, so badly. The idea of taking the literary journal in a fresh new direction filled her with energy and a sense of purpose. She was pretty sure that her biggest competition was Madison Valenzuela. With her straight As, perfect bangs, and impressive vocabulary (she used words like "visceral," which Zinnie had to look up), she commanded attention without ever raising her voice above a cool, inside volume.

And then there was sweet Jenny Tom, who in addition to being a crazy-talented poet, also had a real knack for design. That would come in handy when it came time to create the layout of the journal. Her mother was an art director at a Hollywood studio, and she had taught Jenny how to make her projects and presentations look like something from a magazine. With the help of her mom, Jenny could give *Muses* a new look. And Jenny was also extremely organized. Zinnie felt deflated every time she considered what a natural Jenny was for the job.

But Zinnie also knew that she herself had some special qualities, too. She worked really hard. When other people wrote just two drafts, Zinnie wrote three. In anticipation of the Writers' Workshop trip to England this past spring, Zinnie had researched what routes to take on the Tube, which is what the British call the subway. This way, they were able to set aside the funds they would have used for taxi fares for a traditional high tea in a hotel. Mrs. Lee had told her that she'd taken notice of her work ethic and foresight. Also, Zinnie definitely put the "creative" in "creative writing." She was unafraid to use a bit of magical realism in a story or add what Mrs. Lee called "non-linear narrative structure," meaning telling the story out of order. Mostly, though, there was something about Zinnie that made it easy for her to be friends with everyone. She never hung out with any one group, but could find things in common with lots of girls in her class. She had three simple friendship rules: One, remember everyone's birthday with a funny card. Two, never turn down a nice invitation. And three, be a good listener. The rules were simple and they worked. Even though she was never the most popular or the prettiest or the smartest, kids seemed to like hanging around her. They thought she was funny and nice and a good friend. Would these attributes be enough to get her nominated as a candidate for editor in chief of *Muses*?

Zinnie inhaled deeply and clicked on the link to Jenny Tom's blog. Zinnie held her breath. With an animated backdrop of a wave washing up onto a shore, it looked downright professional. It was called *Poems of Summer*. As Zinnie read the first two entries, she realized that Jenny was going to write a series of poems having to do with summer, presented with supercool graphics, for each post. It was a great idea. So simple and clear, and so Jenny.

Next she looked at Madison Valenzuela's blog. It was called *Sea Change*. Madison was going to write about her summer at the beach in Santa Monica and how much the city of Santa Monica had changed from when her grandmother was a girl by alternating perspectives between her grandmother and herself. She was going to use entries from her grandmother's old diary. She had her grandmother's diary? From when she was Madison's age? *A primary source?* Oh, man. That was so good it hurt. How was Zinnie supposed to compete with a grandmother's diary?

How would she think of a hook with legs? Why were ideas the hardest part?

She took a deep breath as she massaged her temples. Her father had once advised her that if she needed inspiration, she should ask a tree. She stared at the giant beech tree, which a few years ago she'd done a dance around, chanting a plea for help when she was trying to write a play for the talent show. Now she just gazed at its leafy majesty as a breeze fluttered the leaves, and said, "Got any ideas for me, tree?"

She listened to the sounds that followed: leaves rustling, a squirrel scampering across the branches, and a bird warbling, but no blog ideas magically popped into her head. Maybe it was because her stomach was distracting her. A delicious and familiar smell was coming from Aunt Sunny's kitchen window: pancakes! Her mouth started to water. She closed her laptop and pointed at the tree. "I'll check back with you tonight." It was breakfast time! If she didn't come up with something by the end of the day, she thought as she walked toward the house, she was going to use another one of her father's tricks: putting a question—*What should my blog be about?*—on a piece of paper, tucking it under her pillow, and hoping the answer would come in the night.

5 · A Party for Marigold

"Here she is," Aunt Sunny said when Marigold walked into the kitchen the next morning, still bleary from sleep.

It was eight a.m., but only five a.m. in L.A. She might have slept later if the sun hadn't flooded the room with light, her sisters hadn't been so noisy, or the sweet smell of fresh blueberry pancakes drifting up from downstairs hadn't lured her from her bed to the kitchen, where the fan over the stove made a pleasant noise as Aunt Sunny greeted each niece with a kiss on the forehead. Marigold put a hand on her belly as it growled at the sight of the steaming pancakes.

"Where's Tony?" she asked through a yawn.

"Checking for bats!" Lily said.

Lily was rinsing extra blueberries in the sink, and Zinnie was putting plates on the table.

"He'll be down in a jiffy. Now, how many pancakes would you like?" Aunt Sunny asked as she added a few to a pile that she was keeping warm in the oven.

Hmm, Marigold thought. Normally, Marigold drank kale-and-berry smoothies in the morning, but there was nothing—absolutely nothing in the whole world—more irresistible than Aunt Sunny's made-from-scratch silver dollar blueberry pancakes with a hunk of butter melted between them and real maple syrup drizzled on top. Except for maybe Aunt Sunny's surprise brownies. Those were so insanely good that when Marigold got a craving for them back in L.A., she immediately asked her mom if they could whip up a batch together. The ingredients were always on hand in the Silver home. "I think three."

"Sounds a bit modest. I'd better give you four," Aunt Sunny said matter-of-factly. "Would you please help Zinnie set the table? Oh, and we might need extra napkins."

"Sure." Marigold smiled up at her aunt as she opened the silverware drawer and counted out five forks and knives. She was so glad to be back in this kitchen. Even between meals it always smelled like something was cooking in here—pancakes, omelets, roast chicken, baked macaroni and cheese with crispy bread crumbs on top, linguine and clams, scones, cookies, cakes, or brownies. And Aunt Sunny kept the girls busy in here, too. They were forever slicing, measuring, mixing, and of course, washing dishes.

Back home the girls did so many activities and were on such busy schedules that the Silver family rarely ate dinner together. But here at Aunt Sunny's house there was plenty of time for meals, and each one was a group effort.

"I think I'd better start with five pancakes," Zinnie said as she took her seat.

"Me too," Lily said, stuffing a handful of blueberries into her mouth as she plopped onto her chair. "I'm starving!"

Marigold took a bite, and sweet, tangy, buttery deliciousness exploded on her tongue.

"Oh gosh, I hope you've saved some for me," Tony said as he walked into the kitchen. "It's a big job checking for bat droppings. I've worked up quite an appetite."

"You're just in time," Aunt Sunny said as Tony washed his hands. "Five minutes later, and you might have been out of luck."

"Hi, Tony," Marigold said. Zinnie and Lily waved because their mouths were full.

"Good morning, ladies," Tony said before he gave Aunt Sunny a peck and took a seat at the table. As though she could read Marigold's mind, Aunt Sunny slipped one more pancake onto Marigold's plate and then divided the rest between herself and Tony.

"Are we all clear, Tony?" Aunt Sunny asked. Then

she took off her apron and sat across from Marigold.

"This house is officially a bat-free zone," Tony said, and gulped his coffee. "Mighty glad of it, too. Once those little fellas get in, it's not easy to get 'em out."

"They're just trying to project their young," Lily said, her brow furrowed.

Marigold smiled at Lily. Even though the bat had scared Marigold, she was proud of her littlest sister, who had become passionate about science ever since last summer, when she went to camp here in Pruet. It reminded Marigold of herself and how she felt about acting.

"Study bats as much as you like, but let's not let any more into the house," Tony said. "I never did find out, why'd you take the screen off, Marigold?"

"I was, um, just getting some fresh air," Marigold said.

"She was looking for Peter," Lily said, fluttering her eyelashes dramatically.

"I see," Tony said to Marigold. Marigold felt her cheeks burn. She didn't want to discuss her feelings for Peter publicly. For all Marigold knew, he had a girlfriend again this year! And how did Lily know that she had been thinking of Peter? "Young love is a beautiful thing." She could tell Tony wasn't trying to tease her. He was serious, but that made it more embarrassing.

"I told you, I was looking at the stars," Marigold

said, staring at her plate.

"And dreaming of Peter," Zinnie said.

"Guys," Marigold said. She was about to raise her voice and demand that they *leave her alone about Peter*, but then remembered her promise not to fight. Instead, she took a deep breath.

"Last summer I told Peter I'd be his girlfriend," Lily explained to Tony, who nodded solemnly. Lily reached across the table to touch Marigold's hand. "But it's okay. Don't worry, Marigold. I won't get in the way. I know you're in love with him."

"Oh my gosh! I'm not—" Marigold started, and then buttoned her lips. As annoyed as she was, she was also determined to keep the peace. She decided to change the subject. "What else is happening this summer?"

"Aside from the parade, the regatta, the sand castle building contest, and the clambake?" Tony asked with a wink.

"Actually, there is something else happening in addition to all these tricentennial events," Aunt Sunny said. Then she stood up, walked to the bookcase, and picked up a black-and-white photo in a frame. "There's something I've been meaning to share with you."

As she placed the frame on the table, the three sisters leaned in to get a look. Marigold took in the three girls pictured in the photo. She recognized Aunt Sunny immediately. She was the youngest one, with her hair in braids. Her eyes and smile were exactly the same as they were today. In the picture the girls were sitting in a canoe. The older ones were paddling, and Aunt Sunny was sitting in the middle, waving to whoever was taking the picture.

"That's you and your sisters, right?" Marigold asked.

"Exactly. Beatrice and Esther and me," Aunt Sunny said, pointing to each one.

"What a bunch of sweethearts," Tony said. Then he took his glasses out of his shirt pocket and placed them on his nose to get a better look. "You're even prettier today than you were then."

"Oh hush," said Aunt Sunny with a grin, and patted his hand. "Anyway, I was fourteen in this picture."

"My age exactly," Marigold said.

"That's right," said Aunt Sunny. "That's why I'm showing you the photo. In our family it's tradition that on a girl's fourteenth summer, she and her sisters take a canoe up the Pruet River and camp out on Kettle Island. We build a fire, roast marshmallows, tell stories, sing, look at the stars, and celebrate."

"Celebrate what? Her birthday?" Zinnie asked. "That was in March."

"It's a sort of birthday party," Aunt Sunny said. "But more like we're celebrating . . . growing up. Becoming a young woman."

"Like a Bat Mitzvah," Marigold said. A lot of her friends had Bat Mitzvahs. She hadn't because even though their dad was Jewish, she'd never gone to religious school. Whenever she'd asked about what the Bat Mitzvah was for, her parents told her it was about celebrating that the child was "coming-of-age," which was another way to say growing up. Even though Marigold hadn't been interested in religious school, she did think having a party to celebrate growing up sounded fun.

"Or a *quinceañera*," Zinnie said.

Marigold nodded. Other friends of hers, like Pilar, were going to have a *quinceañera*, which was another way to make a big deal about growing up. Pilar had been planning hers for years. She said it was going to be almost as elaborate as a wedding—she'd get to wear a gorgeous dress and long white gloves and get tons of presents.

"That sounds cool," Marigold said. It wasn't until this moment that she realized how much she wanted her own special celebration, because she did feel older this year in some very important way that she couldn't quite put her finger on. And not only that, but her fourteenth birthday had been such a disappointment. It would be especially great if Peter could come along on the camping trip.

"My girls had sweet sixteen parties," Tony said.

"Yes," Aunt Sunny said. "It's a bit like that, but just for family. And less of a party and more of an . . . adventure!"

"Does it have to be just family?" Marigold asked.

 35

"What's wrong with that?" Aunt Sunny asked.

"Yeah," said Lily, crossing her arms.

"It sounds great and everything," Marigold said, not wanting to hurt Aunt Sunny's feelings. "It's just that I already had a family-only party, and it might be fun to include more people."

"But Aunt Sunny wasn't at your party," Zinnie said.

"That's true," Marigold said, smiling at her aunt—though by now she'd already pictured Peter and her looking up at the stars on the banks of a river in the middle of the night!

"The truth is that I'm already breaking tradition by coming along myself," Aunt Sunny said. "But Esther and Beatrice were quite a bit older than me, so it was different. They also knew that river like the backs of their hands, and you've never been there."

"You were an adventurer from the start, weren't you, Sunny?" Tony said.

"Sure was," Aunt Sunny said.

"I don't think your parents would approve of me sending you down the river on your own," Aunt Sunny said.

"So maybe we could break the tradition even . . . a little more?" Marigold asked. "Like by including Peter and his family?"

"Well, now, that's something to consider," Aunt Sunny said. "But really, what I'd love to pass on to you is the sisterly ritual. It's something you'll keep with you for the rest of your lives."

"I understand," Marigold said, but she was disappointed. She was going to have enough time with her sisters this summer in their attic bedroom.

"We'll go swimming, build a campfire, and have s'mores," Aunt Sunny said. "It'll be fun. I promise."

"Let's call it 'the fun fourteenth,'" Zinnie said.

"I like that!" Aunt Sunny said.

"Me too," Marigold said with a smile, because Aunt Sunny seemed really excited about this.

"When are we going on the fun fourteenth?" Lily asked as she picked up her plate to lick off the maple syrup.

"That's a good question," Aunt Sunny said. "Before the tricentennial would be best, I think."

"We could go when there's a full moon," Lily said.

"Definitely," Zinnie said. "All kinds of crazy stuff happens when there's a full moon."

"It affects the ocean's tides," Lily said.

"I'll get the canoe out and make sure it's seaworthy. Or . . . river worthy!" Tony said as he brought his plate and mug to the sink. "I've got to get to work now—we're starting a big job on the other side of the bridge today."

"Heavens. Me, too," Aunt Sunny said, checking her watch. "The Piping Plover Society is creating exhibits for the tricentennial. And I'm also helping the Historical Society organize a tour of the oldest buildings in town. We have a lot of work ahead of us."

"And I need to get to camp," Lily said.

"We'll take you," Marigold said.

"How about you two?" Aunt Sunny asked Marigold and Zinnie. "What's in the works for you today?"

"The beach!" they answered together. One of the best parts about staying at Aunt Sunny's was that they didn't always have to have plans. They could take each day as it came and let it carry them into the evening, like riding a wave into the shore. All Marigold knew was that she wanted to see Peter Pasque as soon as possible. Before she got any more ideas in her head about midnight stargazing or horseback riding, she needed to find out if he had a girlfriend.

"I must say, it's great to see you girls," Tony said as he reached for his hat and headed for the door. "This house comes alive when you're here."

"Quick question," Marigold said before he left the room. "Do you know if the person the town council chooses to be Eliza needs to live in Pruet year-round?"

"I don't see why that would be the case," Tony answered. "Do you know, Sunny?"

"As far as I know there's no rule about that," Aunt Sunny said with a twinkle in her eye.

6 · The Idea Arrives, At Last!

*C*ape Cod food? Tricentennials? True stories about sharing a room the size of a large closet with two sisters?

Zinnie wracked her brain for a blog idea as she and her sisters walked toward town. They were on their way to drop Lily off at camp and then on to the town beach. Zinnie was hoping to see her friend Ashley. A little dramatic and always honest, Ashley cracked her up. And her Massachusetts accent was icing on the cake. Maybe she could help her think of an idea for her blog.

"What am I going to blog about?" Zinnie asked her sisters as they walked toward town. Lily hopped up onto the stone wall and continued walking, balancing as if on a beam. Then she waved to the horses that lived in the pasture, like they were her old friends.

The caramel-colored one swished her tail, and the white one with spots munched on grass.

"Write about the summer in Cape Cod," Marigold said.

"I feel like it needs to be more specific than that," Zinnie said. "I can't just be like, day number one on Cape Cod, day number two on Cape Cod. I need to be more creative!"

"No one else in your class is here," Marigold said. "And we're on the other side of the country. Things *are* different."

"Maybe," Zinnie said, but she wasn't convinced. "But isn't that just like a diary?"

"Isn't that what blogs are?" Marigold asked as a few older kids in Pruet High School T-shirts rode by on bicycles. Marigold stopped to watch them. Lily bent down to study an insect crawling on the stones. In the distance, Zinnie heard hammering and a saw. Someone must have been doing construction. The kids on bikes made a right, disappearing around the bend. "I wonder if those kids are in Peter's class. I wonder what it's like to go to high school here."

"I guess blogs are kind of like diaries," Zinnie said, too focused on the problem at hand to explore this idea with Marigold. "Come on, guys, I really need help. There's nothing special about a plain old diary, even if it is on Cape Cod."

"Write about ladybugs," Lily said as she lowered her

hand to the stone wall and a ladybug crawled onto her finger. Then she slowly climbed off the wall to join her sisters, turning her hand over so that the ladybug settled in her palm.

"What are the other girls writing about?" Marigold asked. Zinnie told them about Jenny's and Madison's projects.

"The grandmother one is a good idea. I bet Aunt Sunny has an old diary," Lily said, watching the ladybug fly away as they rounded the corner.

"I can't do the exact same idea," Zinnie said as the general store, the yacht club, the casino, and Edith's Ice Cream Shop came into view. Edith's wasn't open yet, but Zinnie's stomach groaned at the thought of her delicious ice cream. She wondered what flavors Edith had come up with for the season.

"That'd be copying," Marigold explained to Lily. "Artists need to be original."

"It needs to be something that really gets the readers' attention," Zinnie said. "Hmm. What about an ice cream blog?"

"Bats!" Lily said, turning to Zinnie as if this were the best idea on the planet.

"Bats?" Zinnie asked. Lily nodded. "Well . . . I was thinking, what if that bat bit you and you slowly became a vampire over the summer? That'd make a good blog."

"Creepy!" Marigold said.

"Exactly," Zinnie said.

"Look, vampire bats don't really turn people into vampires. They do survive on blood, which is why people call them that, but they don't live in the United States," Lily said. "Anyway, you don't need to make stuff up! They're the only mammals that can fly. They can live for over thirty years and fly at up to sixty miles per hour! Bats are amazing. That could be the name of your blog—*Amazing Bats*!"

"I'll think about it," Zinnie said. While she could see the vampire idea working for a story or a graphic novel, it didn't seem to be blog material. Besides, after reading all fifteen books in the Fang City series, she was over vampires.

"You could write about love," Marigold said to Zinnie as they passed the yacht club.

"*You* can write about love," Zinnie said, watching as color filled her sister's cheeks.

"Maybe I will," Marigold said, smiling mysteriously as she bent down to pick a wildflower.

She was starting to think that Aunt Sunny was right about the fourteenth year bringing a big change. Marigold seemed to have crossed some invisible line that sometimes felt far away from Zinnie.

"Lots of people want to read about love," Marigold said.

Should I write about romance? Zinnie wondered.

She had liked Max last summer, though she couldn't decide as what. Most of the time, he just felt like a friend. But Zinnie couldn't deny that the idea of seeing him again filled her with a sweet, bright happiness, like a glass of cold lemonade on a hot day.

"I gave you the best idea," Lily said when they arrived at the casino, which was where the Young Naturalists campers met in the morning.

"We'll see you this afternoon," Marigold said, giving Lily a squeeze. "Have fun."

"I will. Bye!" Lily said. She didn't even turn around as she ran to meet her counselors and friends.

"Hey, Ashley!" Zinnie called as soon as they got to the beach. She spotted her old friend right away in her usual spot at the snack stand.

"Zinnie!" Ashley shouted back. Her dark hair was tied up in a ponytail, and she was wearing shorts and a Pruet town beach T-shirt.

As Marigold went to spread her towel on the sand, Zinnie rushed over to say hi to Ashley. "What's up?"

"Just setting up for the day," Ashley said, holding out a red ice pop. "So have a treat on the house and keep me company by telling me one of your funny stories."

"Thanks," Zinnie said as she opened her ice pop. "Get this. Last night a bat flew in the window!"

"A bat?" Ashley asked. "Oh no! Those beady eyes and sharp teeth. And all the germs! Gives me the shivahs!" Zinnie laughed as Ashley said, "Go on. Tell me what happened. I have to know! Did you call an exterminator? Did anyone get bit?" Her eyes widened. "Do you think it had rabies?"

As Zinnie told Ashley the story, she realized that maybe Lily had a point about bats—they were entertaining. Ashley went into a fit of giggles when Zinnie told her about Marigold hiding under the bed, screamed when she told her about the possibility of the bat nesting in Zinnie's curly hair, and cowered by the freezer as Zinnie recounted the moment Lily wrapped the bat in a pillowcase.

"That sounds crazy!" Ashley said. "A real *advencha*. I'd go see that story in the *thea-tah*. You should turn it into a movie."

"Or a blog," Zinnie said, realizing that perhaps Marigold had been right, too. Everyday life in Pruet could be its own hook. There were so many differences between Pruet and Los Angeles. She doubted anyone in her class had heard of hairy cows that wander near beaches or been to a clambake. Maybe she could call her blog *Coast-to-Coast Summer Adventures*. She could compare summer adventures on the East Coast to ones on the West Coast. Yes, that was it! That was the idea she was looking for!

As Ashley took inventory of the granola bars and

Zinnie finished her ice pop, she thought through how this would work. She had to write sixteen posts over eight weeks' time. But she was only in Pruet for a little over two weeks. So, since she wanted the same number of posts for each coast, she'd have to have eight adventures here. That meant she'd have to have to find about four adventures a week! That might be kinda hard. She could start with the bat, anyway, and take it from there. As Zinnie hopped off the stool to help Ashley stock the fridge with sodas, she wondered about that old beech tree. She'd asked it for an idea, and it had delivered yet again. There was clearly something to her dad's advice to "ask a tree" when it seemed like all the good ideas were taken. The thought of him and his round brown eyes and scratchy beard made Zinnie both smile and ache a bit inside. They were going to see their parents the day before the tricentennial, and for just a moment, that felt like an awfully long time.

7 · Peter Pasque

"How was camp?" Marigold asked Lily when they picked her up in the afternoon. After a morning spent swimming at the town beach and browsing at the library, Marigold and Zinnie had returned to Aunt Sunny's for lunch, where Marigold had made them turkey sandwiches. In part to keep time from standing still as she waited to see Peter—the moment was only minutes away now—she'd been silently brainstorming all day about how she could get chosen to represent Eliza Pruet. She kept repeating the words "hardworking," "spirited," and "civic-minded" in her head, hoping an idea would come to her.

"Did you go anywhere cool?" Zinnie asked Lily.

"We went to the marsh and observed some amphibians," Lily said. "And then we made drawings about their life cycles. Did you think of an idea for your blog yet?"

"Coast-to-coast summer adventures," Zinnie said. "I can write about summer in Cape Cod—"

"Like I suggested," Marigold said.

"Yes, and then when we get back to L.A., I can write about how California summers are different."

Marigold smiled. Zinnie always took her advice on clothes, hair, and movies, but she never seemed to ask her opinion about what mattered to her most: her writing. Maybe now that Marigold had been accepted at the Performing Arts Magnet high school Zinnie would come to her for more writing advice.

"I'm going to start by writing about the bats," Zinnie said.

"I told you bats were a good idea," Lily said as they headed over to see Peter.

Marigold tried not to break out into a run—she was just bursting inside to find him. She'd been patient about seeing him all day. Marigold knew from the past two summers that this was the time that sailing practice ended, and she smiled as she saw the small sailboats coming into the harbor and heard the team's voices carrying over the water. She picked up the pace and said a silent prayer that Lindsey wasn't Peter's girlfriend anymore.

"That roof doesn't look so bad," Zinnie said as they approached the familiar building.

"That's because Tony and his crew did a patch-up job to get us through the spring," Mack said.

The sisters turned around to see that Jean and Mack, Peter's parents, had come out to greet them.

"Oh hi," Marigold said.

"Hello, California girls!" Jean said, and gave them a hug.

"Sorry you had such a rough winter," Zinnie said.

"Don't you worry," Mack said. "We have a plan to get everything back into shape. Are you girls excited for the tricentennial?"

"Yes!" said Lily.

"If you need any help, just let me know," Marigold said.

"Here comes Peter," Lily said, pointing toward the docks.

Marigold thought he was as handsome as ever. He was going to be a sophomore in high school, and he looked it. He was taller than last year and was broader, too. And when he smiled right at her, she thought her heart might melt even faster than a scoop of Edith's ice cream in the sun. Even better, Lindsey wasn't anywhere in sight.

"We actually have some big news to share," Jean said. "That's why we came out to meet Peter."

"Big news?" Zinnie asked. "Is it something likely to bring adventure to Pruet?"

"I'd say so," Mack said.

But Marigold was tuning out the conversation as Peter approached.

"How are you?" Marigold asked as she stared into Peter's blue eyes. She couldn't imagine any news more important than knowing that Peter liked her, too. When he smiled back at her, she could tell he did. It was what her mom called her "gut instinct."

"I'm good," Peter said, blushing so much that his freckles almost disappeared. "How are you?"

"Great," Marigold answered.

"We have some news, son," Mack said to Peter as he placed a hand on his shoulder.

"I have some news too," Lily said.

"You go first," Mack said.

"I'm going to be a scientist," Lily said.

"That's great, Lily," Peter said.

"Yes," Lily said. "Except that I don't know if I'll have time for boyfriends. Sorry."

"I understand," Peter said. He winked at Marigold, who smiled back. She always loved how kind Peter was to Lily.

"I can't wait any longer. Let's go get some ice cream," Lily said.

"Good idea," Marigold said. As Peter took a step closer to her, she realized that he smelled like the sea in the best way.

"What about your news?" Zinnie asked Mack and Jean.

Mack started to speak, but Jean cut him off with a nudge.

"You know what?" Jean said. "I think our news can wait until dinner. Let these kids have some ice cream. I don't know if we could get their attention anyway."

Marigold smiled and bowed her head. She knew they were talking about Peter and her. It was embarrassing, but a kind of embarrassing that she didn't mind.

"Good thinking," Mack said. "We'll wait."

"Let's all have dinner together tomorrow night," Marigold said. Her heart was beating double time standing so close to Peter.

"Come to Aunt Sunny's!" Lily said. "We can play hide-and-seek. And she always has so much food."

"Or we can have a picnic at the lighthouse!" Marigold suggested. Watching the sunset from the lighthouse porch would certainly be romantic.

"We'll give her a call," Jean said. "Go get your ice cream, and we'll see you in a bit."

"Okay," Marigold said. Zinnie and Lily ran ahead, both of them dying to get to Edith's. Peter and Marigold exchanged a smile. His teeth were a little crooked, but Marigold liked that. Everyone in L.A. had perfect teeth.

"So, are you ready to have a fun summ-ah?" Peter asked.

Marigold nodded. "So, um, is Lindsey still on the team?"

"She and her family are sailing to Greenland," Peter

said. "For the whole summer."

"Great!" Marigold said. "I mean, that sounds like a cool experience. Lucky her."

"Yeah," Peter said, smiling at her. "It's cool. But for me, I wouldn't miss summer in Pruet for the world."

Then Marigold almost gasped as Peter took her hand. If this was how the summer in Pruet was starting, the next two weeks were shaping up to be the best ever.

8 · New Girl with a Notebook

The smell of waffle cones hit Zinnie at least ten paces before she stepped onto the porch of Edith's Ice Cream Shop. Lily ran ahead of Zinnie to greet Edith's dog, Mocha Chip, who was happily lounging in the sun next to a big bowl of water. His tail thwacked the porch as Lily kneeled down to hug him.

"Your ears are still so soft," Lily said as she nuzzled the dog's neck. "And you still smell like sunshine and"—she leaned in for a good sniff—"chocolate."

"You sure he smells like chocolate?" Peter asked, grinning sweetly at Lily. "I saw him rooting around in the gah-bage out back this morning before practice."

He and Marigold had finally caught up to them and—oh my gosh—Zinnie noticed that they were holding hands, like they were on a date or something!

Marigold's cheeks were pink, and she was smiling so big that it looked like it might hurt, except there were no signs of pain in her eyes, only sparkles of pure delight. Zinnie knew that Marigold wanted Peter to be her boyfriend, but Zinnie didn't think it was going to happen right away, on their very first full day in Pruet. Zinnie wasn't sure why, but she felt a little pang inside her chest. Was Marigold going to want to spend any time with her at all this summer?

She didn't really want to admit this, but she was worried about Marigold going to the Performing Arts Magnet next year. It would be the first time since pre-school that she wasn't in the same school as Marigold. And while they didn't spend that much time together during the day at school, it was nice just knowing she was there. One quick glance at her sister on the playground, and she knew that no matter what happened, she wasn't alone. Marigold sometimes had a funny way of showing it, but Zinnie knew that she was looking out for her.

She hadn't realized it until that moment, but she was going to really miss going to school with Marigold. Performing Arts Magnet was on the other side of town, and Marigold was going to be leaving early in the morning to get there. She'd probably be in plays after school, or she'd have auditions, and Zinnie would be lucky to have any time at all with her sister during the week. No longer would they walk to school together in the mornings, or trade snacks at recess, or sit together in the library during study hall—which only happened about once a month, but still, it meant something to Zinnie. They'd spent more time together than usual this year because of Marigold's falling out with Pilar and the Cuties. Those girls had been so mean to her sister. It had been hard to watch.

Lily had started at Miss Hadley's in kindergarten, and was now going into the second grade this fall, but it was different. First of all, the little kids had a separate playground, so Zinnie didn't see her that much. Second of all, Zinnie and Marigold were only one year apart, so they had grown up together, almost like twins, even though they barely looked related. Lily was so much younger. Little sisters were the ones who needed looking after—they weren't the ones who could save you if something went wrong.

Even though Marigold warned her, Zinnie hadn't believed that seventh grade could be so much different from sixth. But it was. For the most part, Zinnie didn't care about cliques. Unlike Marigold, she was always able to be friends with everyone. It didn't bother her that Emma and Bella Sanderson, who were twins, and Molly Baron had started to stick together so much and were wearing those tight necklaces that Mom said were "so terrible and so nineties." Zinnie had been the one to comfort Molly and loan her some leggings when she wet her pants on a field trip in second grade. After Zinnie had witnessed that, it was pretty impossible to be intimidated by her, even though a lot of the other girls in her class were. Zinnie had seen what Marigold had gone through with the Cuties and hoped it wouldn't happen in her grade. She couldn't imagine it would. The girls in her class were just nicer.

At least she thought so.

Until the first day of class last September. Apparently, over the summer, everyone had made some sort of secret pact to ditch Stuffels, which were the stuffed animals that clipped on to backpacks. They'd been all the rage since third grade, and Zinnie had thought they were adorable. Zinnie had been too wrapped up in her excitement about being part of the Writers' Workshop to notice everyone's backpacks walking into school. But when she'd settled into her math class and Emma and Bella Sanderson had started to laugh, Zinnie had felt the color drain from her face.

"What?" she asked, her throat dry.

"We just can't believe you still like Stuffels," Emma said.

"They're so babyish!" Molly added.

"Do you also wear Pull-Ups at night?" Bella asked, and flipped her hair over her shoulder.

"No!" Zinnie said as, to her horror, most of the class broke out in giggles.

Luckily, they had recess right after math. She ran

straight over to Marigold, who was reading a fashion magazine by the swings.

"I need to talk to you," Zinnie said, and burst into tears.

Marigold took her by the hand and whisked her to the oak tree behind the giant play structure. In the cool shade, Zinnie told her the story in choking sobs. Marigold nodded and listened and then gave her a hug.

"Don't worry," Marigold said. "I got this."

Zinnie watched from behind the tree as Marigold strode over to Molly, Emma, and Bella, who were sitting in a tight circle in the Zen garden their class had created last year. Zinnie held her breath, waiting for Marigold to say something. But she didn't speak a word. She just folded her arms and *looked* at them. With her broad stance and fierce gaze, Marigold was like a cowboy in the Old West. Zinnie could practically see the saloon doors swinging on their hinges and the tumbleweed rolling by. (Their dad was a big fan of Westerns, so Zinnie knew about standoffs.) She watched as Molly, Emma, and Bella seemed to shrink in their skins, their mouths hanging open and their eyes flickering with fear. After a good long stare, Marigold circled them once and then walked back to Zinnie and said, "Let me know if they mess with you again." Then she skipped off back to read her magazine.

"If you like your Stuffels, there's no reason you can't

keep them on your backpack," Marigold said on their way home from school. It was too late. Zinnie had taken them all off during recess and shoved them into the bottom of her gym bag.

"That's okay," Zinnie said. "I'm over them."

"It's not just because those girls were mean to you?" Marigold asked, narrowing her eyes.

"Nope," Zinnie said, then reconsidered. "Maybe it is. But it's not like I like Stuffels that much. I guess I kinda just forgot they were even there."

"I know what you mean," Marigold said. "Some things are worth taking a stand for."

"And other things are just . . . Stuffels," Zinnie said, and they both laughed.

"I can show you how to stencil designs on your bag tonight," Marigold said. "That's what I heard the high school kids are doing, and it looks pretty cool."

"Yeah," Zinnie said. "I'd like that."

Now Zinnie looked at Marigold's and Peter's clasped hands and swallowed hard. Marigold had always been a few steps ahead, but going to a high school on the other side of town and having a boyfriend—that was leaps and bounds into the distance.

"Zinnie, won't you at least smell him?" Lily asked, petting Mocha Chip.

"Sure." Zinnie at least still had Lily. She sniffed

Mocha Chip's head and had to agree. "She's right. This dog smells like chocolate."

"See!" Lily said.

"Maybe that's why Edith named him Mocha Chip," Marigold said. A family of six, who, from their sunburns and messy hair, looked like they'd just spent the day on a sailboat, stepped out of the shop with their cones in hand. "Come on, guys. Let's get in line. All this talk about chocolate is making me hungry," Marigold said.

They walked inside. Marigold and Peter were still holding hands, and Zinnie wondered for a moment if she and Max might hold hands once he arrived in Pruet. Once again she had goose bumps from thinking about Max. And the place was packed. Zinnie recognized some of the kids from her other summers in Pruet. She saw the twins who'd been in her talent show a few years back, and Ashley's dad, who must be on a break from the car dealership. And then she studied the menu, which was written on a chalkboard. Wow! Edith had really gone to town. There were twice as many flavors as last year! There were the classics, like vanilla, mocha chip, peppermint stick, and chocolate. And on the other side of the chalkboard were written all the new and exciting flavors. Zinnie had barely glanced at them when Edith called out to her.

"It's the California kids!" Edith said, reaching over

58

the counter to give the girls a hug. "And Peter, too! How are ya?"

"Great!" Marigold said, still smiling a mile wide.

"Hungry," Lily said.

"Happy to be back," Zinnie said. "You sure are busy today, Edith."

"What do you expect?" Edith said as she wiped her hands on her apron. "I'm unveiling my new flavors today—June 21, the official first day of summer and the longest day of the year."

Edith went back to serving the crowd, and the girls and Peter waited patiently in line until it was their turn, each of them studying the new flavors and silently deciding which one they'd choose.

"Lemon and blackberry bramble?" Zinnie asked when they finally got to the front. "That sounds wonderful."

"It is. With my new flavors, I'm using all local ingredients," Edith said. "After all, it's the town's three hundredth birthday, and I thought it would be nice if my selection was from these parts."

"Can I try a sample of that one, please?" Zinnie asked. "It reminds me of Aunt Sunny's wedding cake."

"That's what inspired it," Edith said, handing her a taste on a tiny spoon. "The berries come from Dean's Farm, just east of here."

"Oh look!" Marigold said, pointing at the sign.

"Sunny's Surprise Brownies is a flavor!"

"Great idea," Zinnie said.

"Aunt Sunny is famous!" Lily said proudly.

"I was wondering who was going to notice first." Edith grinned.

"We all have to try that one," Marigold said, then casting a shy glance at Peter, she added, "Well, at least the three of us do. What'll you have, Peter?"

"Make that four cones of Sunny's Surprise Brownies," Peter said.

Edith got to work preparing the cones, and Zinnie looked around to see if she recognized anyone else. She didn't, but someone caught her eye—a girl sitting in a booth by herself. Something about her hip haircut, with one side a little shorter than the other, and her cool, ripped-on-purpose jeans, which everyone in L.A. was wearing but no one in Pruet was, made her look like she wasn't from Cape Cod.

Despite the hectic atmosphere, the girl was very focused as she wrote in her notebook. This piqued Zinnie's interest. She was dying to know what she was working on. A poem? A play? A journal entry? The girl looked up for a moment and stared out the window, deep in thought. She chewed on her pen for a second, leaning back and tilting her head, as if the answer to a question were written in the sky. Then her eyebrows lifted and she got back to work.

"Here you go, kids," Edith said, handing them their

cones. Marigold slid some money over the counter, and they all tasted their ice cream.

"Yum!" Zinnie said. It tasted a lot like Aunt Sunny's brownies—chocolaty with a peppermint finish, but nothing could be as good as the real ones, straight from Aunt Sunny's oven.

"This is so good I think I'm going to cry," Lily said, and everyone laughed.

"Glad you approve," Edith said. "Now, I'd love to catch up and find out what you've been up to all summer, but I'm hoppin' like a flea on a griddle this afternoon. So come by some morning, and we'll have a longer conversation."

"Bye," Marigold said as she and Peter and Lily all headed outside.

Zinnie lingered. "I know you're busy, but one more thing."

"What's up, buttercup?" Edith asked, holding a finger in the air to give the customer next in line the *one-minute* signal.

"Who's that?" Zinnie asked, gesturing to the girl in the booth. After all, if she was going to have to find another three adventures this week, she had to get started.

Edith gave the girl a long look and then shook her head. "Probably just a summer person. You know, I have people coming over from the Vineyard to try my ice cream."

"She looks . . . interesting," Zinnie said.

"Ask her name," Edith said with a shrug. "Make a friend."

Zinnie thanked Edith and walked toward the booth. The girl's head was bent over her notebook as she sketched something—it looked like she was drawing a comic book panel. Zinnie was about to tap her on the shoulder when she thought better of it. She didn't want to interrupt her. She knew that focused expression—it was that of someone deep in the creative process, and she wasn't going to get in the way. She moved through the crowd and out the door, where she saw her sisters and Peter. She walked as quickly as she could to catch up with them without dropping her ice cream.

9 · Rathbone's News

Marigold basked in the glow around Peter and herself as they walked toward Aunt Sunny's house, eating their ice cream and soaking up the late afternoon sun. It was kind of hard to eat an ice cream cone while holding hands with someone, and their palms were starting to get a little sweaty, but they were managing somehow. Marigold didn't want to let go, and it seemed like Peter didn't want to either, even if it slowed them down. Zinnie and Lily had finished their ice cream a minute or two ago and had run ahead to Aunt Sunny's house to tell the story of how her surprise brownie recipe had become an ice cream flavor. Marigold and Peter were alone for the first time this summer. She was so much in the moment with him that she almost didn't recognize the figure approaching from the opposite direction: Philip

Rathbone, the film director.

As he came closer, Marigold felt her palms tingle with nervousness. She noticed that he was starting to look a little more like a local instead of a famous Hollywood director. He'd ditched his jeans for cotton shorts, his black button-down for a Pruet T-shirt, and his fancy loafers for scuffed-up boat shoes. He was even wearing a Red Sox cap, which was basically part of the local uniform. Peter, who must have noticed that Marigold's palm was getting sweatier by the second, let go of her hand and discreetly wiped his own on the back of his shorts.

"You okay?" he asked.

Marigold nodded.

"Mr. Rathbone," Marigold said as they were about to cross paths. "It's me, Marigold Silver."

"Of course," Mr. Rathbone said as he walked toward them. "I remember you." Marigold smiled and breathed a sigh of relief. She supposed a part of her might never get over the moment when he didn't recognize her last summer after he'd broken her heart by cutting her from a movie. Even though this was their third summer in Pruet, it still amazed Marigold that *the* Philip Rathbone, one of the most successful directors in the world, had a summerhouse nearby. The Silver sisters were used to living near celebrities in Los Angeles. They often saw them around—at the Farmers Market or in the cool vegan restaurant up the street—but because Pruet was so small and special, this was different. This was actually *knowing* one.

Of course the sister who knew him best, the one who he'd never forget, was Zinnie because she had saved his nephew, Cameron, from drowning in the harbor last summer. Marigold had read somewhere that if someone saves the life of a person you love, he or she becomes totally unforgettable. Like, even if you wanted to forget about him or her, you couldn't.

"Nice to see you again, Marigold," Mr. Rathbone said.

"How's Cameron?" Marigold asked.

"He's doing great. He's up in Maine this summer, having a blast at a sleepaway camp."

"Cool," Marigold said. She was about to tell him that she'd been accepted at PAM and was starting next year when Mr. Rathbone turned to Peter.

"Who's your friend?" Mr. Rathbone asked. He smiled at Peter, who was just as tall as he was.

"I'm Peter Pasque," Peter said, extending his hand for a shake.

"No kidding," Mr. Rathbone said as he shook his hand. "You aren't by chance related to Jean and Mack Pasque, are you?"

"They're my parents," Peter said.

"Of course," Mr. Rathbone said. "You look just like your father. How funny to run into you. I was having lunch with your folks just a few hours ago."

"Really?" Marigold asked. She wasn't sure why, but it was hard to imagine the three of them at the same table. Mr. Rathbone was so Hollywood—he looked like he ate nothing but sushi—and Mack and Jean were just so Pruet. She was sure they preferred to eat fish they caught themselves. She tried to imagine what they might talk about.

"They didn't tell me they met a new member today," Peter said. "We don't get a lot of new members around here. It's pretty much the same crowd year after year. What kind of boat do you have? A schooner? A sloop?"

"Oh, I don't know the first thing about sailing," Mr. Rathbone said. "And I don't have a boat because I get seasick."

"Then why'd you join the yacht club?" Peter asked.

"I didn't join the club. I'm renting it out for next ten days. I'm directing a new TV show, and when the writers came up with the idea of an episode that takes place in a seaside town, I thought that Pruet was the perfect place to set it—and film it."

"How exciting!" Marigold said.

"It is," Mr. Rathbone said. "Pruet is an ideal location. There was another spot up on the Cape that was going to let us use their yacht club, but then my niece told me that she thought this was a much better location. And she was right. It is."

"This doesn't make any sense," Peter said. "Will you just be using the yacht club, like, before it opens in the mornings or something?"

"We'll be using it all day, every day, for ten days," Mr. Rathbone said.

"That can't be right," Peter said. Marigold watched as his neck turned red. "See, the yacht club is where our sailing team practices. We have races all the time. Our tricentennial regatta is in two weeks. How are we going to win if we have nowhere to practice?"

Marigold noticed that his accent seemed more pronounced.

"Hmm. I don't know," Mr. Rathbone said. "Your parents didn't seem concerned about this."

"I just don't see why they would rent it out now," Peter said as he played with the bill of his Red Sox cap.

"I don't know what to tell you except that when I made my offer, your parents assured me that it would not only cover the lost business, but allow them to do some much-needed construction on the roof," Mr. Rathbone said. He tilted his head and was smiling, as if to offer an apology to Peter, but Peter's brow furrowed and his jaw flexed. "I know the storms here this winter were brutal and definitely took their toll."

"Um, maybe you can still use the docks? You won't need the docks all the time. Right, Mr. Rathbone?" Marigold asked hopefully. But he just shook his head.

"Not all the time. I'll have to check the production schedule. Hopefully, we won't cause too much trouble for you, Peter." Mr. Rathbone shifted his stance. He was starting to look uncomfortable. "Anyway, I have to run. I'm actually meeting my producers at the yacht club right now."

Peter stood totally still, and Marigold could feel frustration wafting off his body.

"One more thing," Marigold said to Mr. Rathbone as he was walking away. "Will you be doing any casting here?" She knew her question would probably annoy Peter, but she just had to ask.

"Yes. Mostly extras, but a few speaking parts, too. I know there are some professionals here." He winked at her. "And I want to help the community as much as possible."

With that, he turned around and headed toward the yacht club.

"'Help the community'? Gimme a break. What about our regatta? And where are people supposed to keep their boats if he's using the docks, too?" Peter asked. His voice had an edge to it that made Marigold's stomach knot up.

Marigold was caught between two feelings. She was empathizing with Peter, who was clearly distraught, while at the same time tingling with excitement at the prospect of acting for Mr. Rathbone and being on a set.

"There's no way this is true," Peter said, shaking his head.

"It's only for ten days," Marigold offered.

"During summer!" Peter said.

"I'm sure your parents have a plan," Marigold started.

"This is awful," Peter said. He threw his ice cream into a nearby trash can. "I need to talk to them."

"Peter, wait!" Marigold said, her ice cream dripping all over her fingers.

"I gotta go," he said, and broke into a run.

10 · A Moment with Aunt Sunny

"**A**re the creative juices flowing this morning?" Aunt Sunny asked the next day as she emerged from the back door carrying two mugs of coffee. Zinnie was sitting at the picnic table under the tree, putting the final touches on her first blog post. "The Great Bat Caper," as she'd titled it, had been a fun post to write. She'd actually made herself laugh as she typed, recalling Marigold's shrieks and Lily's annoyance at her sisters' reactions to the "poor, innocent bat."

As she hit "publish," she smiled up at Aunt Sunny, who was still in her bathrobe. She placed the two mugs of coffee in front of them. It wasn't real coffee—which is what her mom called the kind with caffeine. This was Aunt Sunny's special morning drink, which she made both for herself and Zinnie: half decaf coffee and half warmed-up milk, with two generous teaspoons of sugar, stirred well, with a sprinkle of cinnamon on top.

"You look triumphant," Aunt Sunny said as the early morning light filtered through the leaves of the beech tree. The neighborhood was starting to wake up. More birds joined the chorus, and in the distance Zinnie heard a lawn mower.

"I just published my first post," Zinnie said, and sipped the delicious coffee.

"That is a triumph," Aunt Sunny said. "Since you're finished, may I join you?"

"Of course," Zinnie said. She loved how Aunt Sunny always treated her writing as though it were just as important as any other person's work.

"Tell me about this project," Aunt Sunny said. "You started to yesterday, but we were interrupted when Marigold arrived with the big news about Mr. Rathbone."

Zinnie was surprised when Marigold had come home so quickly yesterday, especially since it seemed like she and Peter would want at least a few hours to stare into each other's eyes. If Max were her boyfriend, would they do that too?

"I still can't believe that Mr. Rathbone will be shooting scenes for his TV episode at the yacht club," Aunt Sunny said. "Jean says Peter is not happy about it. But anyway, I want to know what you've been writing about. Tell me, what is the theme of your blog?"

"I'm going to be comparing summer on the East Coast to summer on the West Coast. My idea is that each post will be about a summer adventure I have, first here and then in L.A.," Zinnie told Aunt Sunny. "But because we're only here for about two weeks, I need to have four adventures a week. I've got the first one down, but I'm a little worried about trying to have so many adventures in such a short period of time. I'm hoping the adventures will find me, like the way the Great Bat Caper did, but I think I might need to seek them out somehow."

"I see what you mean," Aunt Sunny said, taking a thoughtful sip of her coffee. "Let's think about this. I'm sure Mr. Rathbone's TV episode will drum up some action."

Zinnie nodded. "I couldn't stop thinking about headlines last night. Like, 'L.A. Meets Pruet,' 'Sailing into Hollywood,' 'Big Lights in a Small Town.'"

"You're a born writer," Aunt Sunny said. "And then, of course, there's the fun fourteenth." Aunt Sunny's face broke into a huge smile. "Three intrepid sisters and their trusty aunt Sunny take to the river in a great family tradition!"

"True," Zinnie said. There was bound to be adventure on the fun fourteenth. She could tell that Marigold wasn't that excited about it, so Zinnie was going to be extra enthusiastic. The fun fourteenth clearly meant a lot to Aunt Sunny, and the idea of hurting her feelings was too terrible to contemplate. Zinnie was determined to have enough eagerness for both herself and Marigold—she'd learned how to make a fire and pitch a tent during her wilderness weekend in the Angeles National Forest, and she was ready to show off her skills. "It's going to be so great! I can't wait!"

"Me either," Aunt Sunny said. "And then the tricentennial, of course! That's four posts right there."

"But what about the others?" Zinnie asked. "I can't just wait for adventures to find me. Do you have any ideas for places I could go looking for some?"

"I'm sure I can think of something. But we need more minds on this task. I can spread the word," Aunt Sunny said.

"Edith can help," Zinnie said, the idea coming to her with pleasing speed.

"And maybe people can email you with suggestions," Aunt Sunny added.

"That would be awesome," Zinnie said, sighing with relief. Aunt Sunny knew everyone in Pruet, and with more people brainstorming, four additional adventures felt more than possible. They felt inevitable.

11 · Sunshine of the Night

"Aha!" Aunt Sunny said, holding a red lantern out for Marigold. "I knew I'd find it if I looked hard enough! Isn't it a beauty?"

"Yes, it's so cool and . . . vintage," Marigold said, mustering up as much enthusiasm as she possibly could for an old camping lantern.

"My sisters and I called this lantern 'sunshine of the night,' because it shone so brightly for us," Aunt Sunny said wistfully.

They were in the kitchen, where Marigold had just put a batch of peanut butter cookies into the oven. Zinnie and Lily were in town picking up some ice cream to go with the cookies for dessert, and Tony was outside grilling the fish he'd caught that afternoon. Peter's family was coming over for a picnic tonight, and Marigold was hoping the cookies might cheer him up about the yacht club.

"It hasn't seen the light of day in thirty years, but I bet with a little TLC, we'll have it working in no time," Aunt Sunny said, gazing at the lantern as if it was made of gold instead of rusty metal.

"Awesome," Marigold said.

"Just the sight of this lantern fills me with memories of my sisters, and now I get to pass it on to you," Aunt Sunny said, wiping off the dust with a dish cloth. "As the girl of honor, you'll be the one to guide the rest of us."

"I can't wait," Marigold said a little too loudly. She was trying hard to appear enthusiastic for Aunt Sunny, but she was having a hard time getting excited about her fun fourteenth. In fact, she was dreading it.

Camping wasn't her thing. Zinnie was the one who was into it. Marigold preferred to sleep indoors, in a bed, and with a bathroom nearby. What was so great about sleeping outside?

"Where will we, um, go to the bathroom?" Marigold asked.

"We'll dig a latrine," Aunt Sunny said, as if this were no big deal.

"Okay." *Oh no*, thought Marigold, and she smiled even more broadly to cover up her disgust. Since the whole idea was to celebrate her growing up, shouldn't she have a say in this? "I have an idea," she said as Aunt Sunny cleaned off the various small parts of the lantern. "Wouldn't it just be easier if we camped in the backyard? We could still roast marshmallows there, right? And I hate for you to go to all this trouble."

"It's no trouble at all!" Aunt Sunny said as she used some Windex to clean the lantern's glass sides. "I've been looking forward to this ever since I had the idea this spring. You deserve to be celebrated, and I think you'll love the river. There's something about this ritual that is deeply enlightening. Sometimes we need to take a journey to find what we didn't even know we were looking for."

"Oh," Marigold said. The only thing that would make this truly fun, she thought, was if Peter could come, too. To sit under the stars with Peter, late into the evening, would be awesome. In fact, it would be totally unforgettable.

"Anyone home?" Jean called from the hallway. "It smells heavenly in here!"

"We're in the kitchen," Aunt Sunny called back. Marigold's heart beat faster in anticipation of spending time with Peter, who she hadn't seen since they'd run into Mr. Rathbone yesterday. She was really hoping he would hold her hand again. "Check out what I've unearthed!"

"Hi," Marigold said as the Pasque family walked into the kitchen. Jean was carrying a green salad, Mack held a couple bottles of sparkling water, and Peter trailed behind with a potato salad. One look at his pale face told Marigold that he was still distraught. "I'm making peanut butter cookies."

"Cool," Peter said, and smiled, but Marigold couldn't feel his smile the way she usually could. Normally, the sight of it spread sparkles to her fingers and toes. But tonight it was as if something inside him had been tamped down. Was it just his disappointment over the yacht club, or had he for some reason decided he didn't like her anymore?

"Peter, remember what we talked about," Jean said as she placed the salad on the counter.

"I'm trying," Peter said. He handed the potato salad to his mom and then took a seat at the kitchen table.

"Have some of these fresh berries," Aunt Sunny said, offering him a bowl.

"I'm not really hungry," Peter said. "But thank you."

"Are you okay?" Marigold asked, sitting across from him.

"I just think this whole thing is a big mistake," Peter said. Jean and Mack exchanged a glance.

"We've been over this, Peter," Jean said. "Renting out the yacht club to Mr. Rathbone will allow us to build that extra dock and make that repair to the roof—the damage done this winter was severe, and we don't want to raise membership costs to cover it. We'd risk losing some of our favorite members. The Pruet Yacht Club should be a place for the community, not just our very wealthy summer residents."

"Exactly!" Peter said. "But we're keeping out the locals right now!"

"Only for ten days," Mack said.

"The summer people don't even usually show up until the middle of July, and they think they're so great, but they don't bring anything to Pruet except their attitudes," Peter said.

"We only visit in the summer," Marigold said. "Does that go for us, too?"

"Of course not," Jean said.

"I don't get it," Marigold said. "What's so bad about summer people?"

"Nothing," Mack said with a sigh.

"But there can be some tension," Aunt Sunny said, placing a hand on Peter's shoulder.

"Most of the people who come in the summer have a lot more money than the locals," Mack said. "And some of them, well, treat us . . ."

"Like they're better than us," Peter said. "But the truth is that we're the people who make Pruet great, the people who are here all year. All the kids who play on the sports teams and make leaf piles in the fall and shovel snow in the winter and help their parents clean out the gutters in the spring. The summer people just show up in their fancy boats after we've worked hard all year and act like they own the place. And the Hollywood people? Forget it! They're even worse."

Marigold swallowed hard. She seemed to be in both of these groups.

"And anyway," Peter continued. "The only people you're hurting right now are the ones in this community. Besides, I thought we were going to have a fund-raiser for the roof."

"Peter, dear, I've been over the numbers myself. The amount of money Mr. Rathbone is paying is worth three of our fund-raisers," Aunt Sunny said.

"You can still use the docks and go sailing, right?" Marigold asked.

"Only if his 'production schedule' allows for it. How am I supposed to prepare if I can't practice for hours a day? Do you know how embarrassing it's going to be if Pruet loses our own tricentennial regatta? It's not fair," Peter muttered under his breath.

"Peter, you're just going to have to make the best of it," Mack said.

Peter didn't roll his eyes, but it looked like he wanted to.

"How about some positive news?" Jean said. "Sirens and Sailors are going to play on the yacht club lawn right after the regatta!"

"Wow!" Marigold said.

"Who are they?" Aunt Sunny asked.

"Who are Sirens and Sailors?" Marigold said. "They are like one of the coolest indie bands out there. How

 79

did you get them to come to Pruet, Jean?"

"They graduated from Pruet High about five years ago. Can you believe it?" Jean said. "They'll bring the whole town out for the celebration."

"That's really cool," Marigold said.

Zinnie and Lily flew in the doorway, holding the ice cream from Edith's.

"Guess what?" Zinnie said. "When we were in Edith's there was an announcement on the radio that Mr. Rathbone is having an open call tomorrow."

"That means anyone and everyone can audition," Marigold explained. Her heart picked up its pace at the thought.

"They're casting extras and three speaking parts," Lily added.

"A waitress, a dock boy, and a fisherman," Zinnie said.

Within a second, images of waitresses flipped through Marigold's mind. She knew in a moment she'd wear a white oxford shirt and her hair in a loose ponytail.

"Peter, you should try out for the dock boy," Lily said.

"Nah, I don't think so," Peter said, and shook his head.

"Maybe Tony will be the fisherman!" Lily added gleefully as Aunt Sunny put the ice cream in the freezer.

"Let's go tell him about it," Zinnie said. And they ran out as quickly as they had arrived.

"Marigold and Peter, will you go pick some flowers for the table tonight?" Aunt Sunny asked. "I'm thinking some of those forget-me-nots by the beech tree would look nice."

As Marigold and Peter strolled through the pear orchard, she hoped Peter might take her hand, but he didn't.

12 · Auditions

"Wow, check out this line!" Marigold said as she, Zinnie, and Lily walked into town the next morning. They were on their way to take Lily to camp when they saw that the line to audition for Mr. Rathbone's TV show stretched all the way down Harbor Road. Word about the open call had spread, and the rest of the town clearly didn't feel the way Peter did.

"Break a leg!" Lily said when they dropped her off with the Young Naturalists. She was much more interested in the bird's nests they were going to study at camp than the equipment trucks that were taking up half the road or the hopeful people who had come to audition. Some had brought beach chairs and coolers. Family members were saving spots and taking turns to use the bathroom and get snacks.

"I guess Hollywood really has come to Pruet,"

Zinnie said as they took their place at the back of the line. Zinnie pulled her notebook out of her pocket and started to jot something down—probably for her blog.

"I guess so," Marigold said, scanning the line for Peter. It was crazy to think he'd change his mind after how adamant he'd been last night, but she still held out a bit of hope that he'd come around and audition. Mostly, she just wanted him to be in a good mood again—a handholding mood. "I bet this wait is going to be hours long. Look, isn't that your friend from the snack shack?"

"Ashley, what's up?" Zinnie said.

"I'm auditioning," Ashley said. "You may remember I won the talent show a few years back."

"Hi, Ashley," Marigold said. "Hey, how about you two save our spots, and I'll run back to Aunt Sunny's and get us some beach chairs."

"Sounds like a plan," Ashley said.

"And maybe some snacks, too," Zinnie said.

Marigold had just crossed Harbor Road when she saw Jean, clipboard in hand, looking harried. Suddenly she had a great idea.

"Jean, I'd love to be your assistant," Marigold said. "I'm really good at organizing stuff, and I know you're going to need a lot of help."

"Perfect!" Jean said. "I could really use it."

This would prove to Peter that she wasn't just a summer person! And it would also be very civic-minded of her. Marigold was going to turn this situation around. Having Mr. Rathbone take over the yacht club for a little while wasn't going to be as bad as Peter thought.

"My name is Marigold Silver, and I'm auditioning for the part of waitress," Marigold said into the camera. This was called "slating," and she'd done it many times before. Still, it was weird to be auditioning right here in the Pruet Yacht Club, in Jean and Mack's office, with a casting director named Meg, Philip Rathbone, and a girl with an asymmetrical haircut running the camera.

"Okay, Marigold," Meg said, handing her a tray with a coffee cup on it. "Why don't you use these props and then go ahead and read the line for me. You can pretend I'm the customer."

"Here's your coffee," Marigold said, saying the line and pretending to be Maggie, the Silver family's regular waitress at her favorite breakfast spot in L.A., the Freeway Café. She had decided in advance that she was a busy but polite waitress who was saving for college tuition. With so many tables to serve, this waitress didn't have time to chitchat.

Acting was actually a lot like writing, Marigold had thought as she was preparing for her audition in the pear orchard last night—the more she made up stories for the characters she was playing, the more she was able to really pretend she was someone else. She gave a curt but professional smile to Meg, and then in a moment that felt like a stroke of genius, cleared a plate that had some crumbs on it, which Meg had obviously actually used for her own breakfast. "Scuse me," Marigold improvised, and turned away from the camera.

"Brava!" Meg said, jotting down some notes. The girl with the asymmetrical haircut turned off the camera. "Well done, Marigold!" Meg continued with a smile that told Marigold she'd at least be getting a callback. "Though I see by your résumé that you have some real credits."

"She's a pro," Mr. Rathbone said, and winked at her.

"Thank you," Marigold said, beaming inside. She'd done a good job; she could feel it.

"Should I go get the next person?" the girl behind the camera asked.

"Sure," Mr. Rathbone said.

"Okay," the girl with the asymmetrical haircut said. Marigold knew exactly who was next—Zinnie.

"I'll go with you," Marigold said. "My sister is next in line."

"Thanks," the girl said as they walked out of the office and through the dining room, where production assistants were taking measurements and clearing out the yacht club furniture to bring in their own. "I'm

Chloe, by the way. I'm Philip's niece."

"Cameron's cousin?" Marigold asked. Chloe nodded. "Were you here last summer?"

"No, I was doing a filmmaking program in New York," Chloe said.

"That's so cool," Marigold said. "Because my sister was the one—"

"Your sister is Zinnie!" Chloe said, her face brightening. "My family loves her. I really want to meet her."

"I can introduce you right now," Marigold said as the girls walked out the entrance and made their way to the start of the line in the driveway. "Do you live in New York?"

"I wish! New York is so cool," Chloe said. "I live in L.A."

"I do too!" Marigold said. "Where do you go to school?"

"I was at Bright Path, but I'm starting at Performing Arts Magnet next year," Chloe said.

"What?" Marigold asked, touching Chloe's hand without even thinking about it. "Me too!"

"Awesome," Chloe said.

Marigold couldn't believe her luck. Here was the possibility of her first high school friend, right here in Pruet. And this girl was *cool*. She had great style, and she knew how to use a movie camera. Oh my goodness,

Marigold thought, remembering a few nights ago when she'd wished for a friend on a star. Here she was—an honest-to-goodness wish come true! Maybe they could work on projects together—maybe they could make their own movies as a team!

"I don't know anyone else who got in," Chloe said.

"Me either," Marigold squealed, happier than ever that she was going to PAM. There weren't going to be any Cuties there. There would just be other artists like Chloe. And now she'd get to go to school knowing someone!

Marigold pointed out Zinnie, who was waiting in line with Ashley. Zinnie's face was alive the way it was when she was doing an impersonation and Ashley was laughing. Meanwhile, Edith was racking up customers by the minute. She was taking orders from the sidewalk and making change with dollar bills and coins from her apron pockets.

"My sister is kind of a spaz," Marigold warned Chloe as she pointed her out.

"She's funny!" Chloe said as Zinnie did what looked like a zombie walk. What was Zinnie talking about, Marigold wondered.

"Zinnie, this is Chloe," Marigold said. "She's Mr. Rathbone's niece, and she's also running the camera for the auditions. And you're next."

"Hi," Zinnie said.

"I'm so happy to meet you," Chloe said, embracing Zinnie in a bear hug. "You don't know me, but I know you."

"Really?" Zinnie asked.

"You saved my little cousin last year," Chloe said. "I can never thank you enough."

"You're welcome," Zinnie said. "And actually, I know who you are, too."

"You do?" Chloe asked.

"Yeah, you're the notebook girl," Zinnie said.

Marigold felt her brow furrow. What was Zinnie talking about?

"My sister has a wild imagination—" Marigold started, but Chloe didn't look surprised at all.

"Wait, you saw me writing in my notebook?" Chloe asked.

"Yes," Zinnie said. "In Edith's." Zinnie pulled her own notebook out of her pocket. "And you know what? I'm a notebook girl, too."

Marigold felt a sting of jealousy. When Marigold and Pilar were still best friends, she worried that Pilar liked Zinnie better than her. When they all hung out together, Pilar would laugh at Zinnie's jokes, and she would invite Zinnie to go shopping with them when Marigold would have preferred some one-on-one time with her friend. Was that going to happen with Chloe? It couldn't, she remembered, because Zinnie would be at Miss Hadley's, and Marigold and Chloe would be all the way on the other side of town at PAM.

"Come on," Chloe said, leading Zinnie back to the yacht club office. "It's time for you to audition."

13 · The Wrong Accent

The next morning before her sisters woke up, Zinnie grabbed some orange juice, a blueberry muffin, and her laptop and headed out to her picnic table to get to work. She'd received an email from Mrs. Lee last night, confirming that it was okay for Zinnie to complete her first eight posts in such a short period of time.

I wish you luck on this ambitious project, Mrs. Lee had written. *Producing eight quality posts in two weeks will be a challenge, but I have faith in you.*

The word "quality" had been circling in Zinnie's mind as she'd drifted off to sleep. Of course she wanted to turn in her best work—she always wanted to do that—but the fact that Mrs. Lee had mentioned it in the email reminded Zinnie of just how hard this task was. With only two posts a week, her classmates would have several days to compose and refine their posts. Zinnie, on the other hand, was going to have to work much more quickly without sacrificing excellence. She hoped Aunt Sunny was right about Edith spreading the word about her blog.

She'd also checked on her classmates' blogs again last night—and they were so good; even better than Zinnie had anticipated. Madison's dual diary blog had almost moved Zinnie to tears! Jenny Tom's designs looked fantastic. And then Sophie Hamilton was spending the summer in Washington, DC, following her aunt who was a congresswoman. Her first blog posts were linked to articles about current events. Zinnie just had one post—about bats, of all things. She was determined to knock it out of the park this morning.

Sitting cross-legged on the bench, she got right to work. Luckily, she knew exactly what she was going to write about: her audition! It had not gone well, but instead of making it about not getting something she wanted, she was going to give it a comic spin.

She laughed to herself, remembering just how determined she was to do a Massachusetts accent. She'd been practicing in line with Ashley, who was coaching her to say "Hee-ah's yah cuppa caw-fee," not "Here's your cup of coffee." She thought she had it down. Ashley had given her the thumbs-up.

When it was Zinnie's turn, Chloe had brought her into the room and introduced her. Mr. Rathbone had beamed at her from behind the desk and said, "As if this one needs any introduction!" Zinnie smiled as Chloe explained to the casting director the story of Zinnie saving Cameron last summer.

The casting director gave Zinnie some directions about carrying the tray and using the props. Chloe prepared the camera, and then said, "Okay, go ahead and slate." Zinnie said her name and then took a deep breath to get into character. The casting director called "Action!" Feeling that she had to move fast in order to keep everyone's attention, she practically sprinted toward the table with the coffee and then, skidding to a stop, said, "Here's your cup of tea" in a British accent! British! Ugh! She guessed this was inevitable because after the Writers' Workshop trip to England in the spring, British accents were hands down her favorite. Zinnie could hear the words coming out of her mouth wrong, but she couldn't seem to stop them. And even worse than the accent was the fact that she totally messed up the line. She'd said "tea" instead of "coffee"!

There was a long and awkward silence in the room. The casting director, a lady who seemed entirely out of place in Pruet with her professional hair and makeup, looked like she was trying very hard not to laugh.

"That was . . . interesting," she'd said, and pursed her lips. "Thank you for coming in."

Mr. Rathbone smiled awkwardly and said, "If we

were looking to cast a lifeguard, you'd be our first choice, Zinnia."

Zinnie's heart sank, because she could feel how nice he was trying to be, and that meant she certainly didn't get the part. Even though she knew she didn't stand a chance against her naturally talented sister, especially after saying the wrong line in the wrong accent, a teeny-tiny part of her had dared to hope. That same small part of her had then gone beyond hoping to getting excited about the idea of being on a TV show.

"Do you think I could try that again?" Zinnie asked. She'd waited hours to audition. She should at least give it her best shot. "See, I went to England this past year, and I have this British accent stuck in my head. If I could have another chance, I'd really appreciate it. I know I'll get it right the second time."

"For the girl who saved Cameron's life?" Mr. Rathbone said. "How could I say no?"

"Thank you so much," Zinnie said. "I promise I can sound just like a Cape Cod native."

"Just relax and be yourself," the casting director said. "And have fun with it."

"Okay," Zinnie said. "No problem." Then she inhaled a deep breath and rolled her neck. Gathering her props, she took a few steps away from the table to her original starting position. *Massachusetts accent, Massachusetts accent,* she thought, silently reviewing how Ashley had taught her to pronounce the words: *Hee-ahs ya cuppa cawfee.*

"Are you ready?" the casting director asked.

"I'm ready," Zinnie said.

"Okay then, we're rolling," Chloe said.

"Action!" Meg said.

Once again, Zinnie took purposeful strides toward the table, ready to be the best dang waitress these people had ever seen!

"Here's your cup of tea," Zinnie said boldly, in an accent that wasn't British or Massachusetts. It was Southern! And she'd gotten the line wrong again! "Did I say 'tea'? I mean 'coffee.'" She was sounding more like a sassy girl from the South with every syllable! "Coffee's what we serve here! No tea for us! In fact, if it's tea you want, you'd better skedaddle!" Oh gosh, what was happening? Her mouth seemed to have a mind of its own! But out of the corner of her eye, she saw that Mr. Rathbone was smiling. Maybe he liked this Southern waitress! She kept going. "There's no tea in these here parts. Just good American coffee. As strong as the day is long! In fact, I'm going to pour myself a mug right now." She picked up the mug, and in her enthusiasm, spilled it down her shirt.

"Whoa. Are you okay?" Meg asked.

"Yes," Zinnie said, feeling her face burn with embarrassment. Her shirt, stained with coffee, clung to her body.

"Well," Meg said as she handed her a paper towel. "That was even more . . . interesting."

For a moment Zinnie wished the floor would just swallow her up. Her heart was pounding in her chest, and she could feel her T-shirt sticking to her lower back where she'd been sweating. It had taken a lot of courage to ask to audition again, and it had only served to make her look like a total idiot! She swallowed, but her mouth was completely dry.

"I liked it," Chloe said cheerfully.

"Really?" Zinnie asked, pulling her shirt away from herself.

"Yeah," Chloe said. "You made me laugh. I think I have an extra shirt in my bag if you want to borrow one."

Zinnie smiled back at her. There was something about kindness coming so swiftly after humiliation that made it that much sweeter.

"That's okay," Zinnie said. "I'm going to the beach after this so I'm about to change into my bathing suit anyway."

"You've brightened our day, Zinnie," Mr. Rathbone said.

"I'm happy to help in any ol' way I can," Zinnie said in a purposeful Southern accent this time. Mr. Rathbone, Chloe, and even Meg chuckled. Zinnie curtsied and added a "toodle-oo!" on her way out the door.

Unable to stop smiling, and wondering if perhaps

she'd changed their minds just a little with this flamboyant good-bye, she waited for Ashley to finish her audition. When Ashley wandered out of the building, also smiling, the two of them went to the town beach, where the snack bar had a sign hanging on it: "Back after TV audition."

"Like I told you before," Ashley had said when they'd taken a shortcut through the library's garden. "Whenever you come to town you bring adven-cha!"

Zinnie tried to capture every detail in her blog post. She paused for a moment as she typed, "It's funny how everything can go wrong and yet feel exactly right." She buzzed a little as she read that line over, simply because it felt so true. She had found the words that matched the experience—and none of them were what Mrs. Lee called "ten-dollar words." Just plain, simple language.

She checked her email one more time, and to her delight there was a message from Max in her inbox. She felt herself break out in a huge smile. She'd be seeing him so soon!

Hey, Zinnie,

Italy is awesome, but I can't wait to be back in Pruet. I have a surprise, but I'm going to wait until I see you to tell you what it is. So hope you enjoy a good mystery, haha.

See you soon,

Max

"Whatever you're reading must be really good," Marigold said, standing in front her with her hands on her hips.

- "It's just an email," Zinnie said. Her heart skipped as she shut her laptop. The email she'd just read was definitely good! Max had something to tell her—something possibly mysterious—and that filled her with a delightful anticipation. She didn't want to share this with Marigold, not yet anyway, because she just wasn't ready to be teased about it. So she quickly changed the subject to one of Marigold's favorites—clothes. "Nice outfit!"

"Thanks."

Marigold did look awesome. She was wearing white shorts, a French-style striped shirt, and gold Sperry Topsiders. She had a crisp canvas tote, with blue handles and her monogram. She looked like she'd created an inspiration board to come up with this outfit: nautical chic. Zinnie also noticed that she had a muffin wrapped in a paper towel.

"Where are you going?" Zinnie asked.

"I'm helping out Jean with the tricentennial, remember? There's so much to do. She really needs a good assistant. Like me," Marigold said. If there was one thing Zinnie's sister loved as much as acting, it was organizing. She liked making lists and checking things off and being prepared.

"I can help too," Zinnie said.

"Great," Marigold said. "I'm going to be so busy as her assistant that I'll probably need an assistant of my own."

"Ha-ha, very funny," Zinnie said good-naturedly. This was normally the kind of comment that would get under Zinnie's skin, but after getting that email from Max, it would take more than a bossy remark from Marigold to sink her spirits.

"See you there at nine? By that time I should have a list of stuff for us to do. Oh, and Mr. Rathbone isn't using the little back room that's behind the kitchen, so that's tricentennial headquarters."

"I'll be there as soon as I can," Zinnie said. As Marigold walked down the driveway, Zinnie opened her laptop and reread Max's email about twenty more times. There was no doubt about it anymore—she *liked* him liked him.

14 · The Perfect Assistant

Marigold hardly recognized the yacht club parking lot. There were several equipment trucks for Mr. Rathbone's production, as well as trailers, which Marigold recognized as being mobile dressing rooms for the actors. She felt a shiver run through her at the possibility that she might be in the cast—at least she would be if her audition went as well as she thought it had.

Was Chloe here now? Marigold looked around but didn't see her—at least not yet. The yacht club wasn't very big at all, and she was bound to run into her before long. If she saw Chloe today, she was going to ask her if she wanted to go to Edith's with her some afternoon this week. They had so much to talk about, like if Chloe had liked middle school, and why she'd applied to Performing Arts Magnet, and what her concentration was going to be. At PAM, students were allowed to choose an area of focus, like dance, acting, or music. Marigold was obviously choosing acting, and she hoped Chloe was, too.

She also wondered if she might catch sight of Daryl Johnson, the star of the show and a major Hollywood actor. Of course, she would play it cool if she did see him. As an L.A. actress, she knew better than to ask stars for autographs. It was considered uncool, even though Marigold had never understood why. When she was a famous actress, she would definitely be happy to give out her autograph. Marigold made her way past a bunch of crew members drinking coffee and discussing the day's schedule, and through the back entrance of the yacht club, which led to the small room where she was meeting Jean.

"Thank goodness you're here," Jean said, greeting her with a smile. The room was tidy, with a desk and two chairs, a filing cabinet, and a window with a view of the harbor. Marigold scanned the docks to see if Peter was anywhere in sight, but he wasn't. "Mack and I have a meeting with the clambake committee in fifteen minutes, and there's so much to accomplish today." She gestured to a chair and handed Marigold a notebook and a pen. "Are you ready to take some notes?"

"Absolutely," Marigold said. "I love making lists. Oh, and I brought you a muffin in case you needed some extra energy."

"You're doing a great job already," Jean said as Marigold reached into her bag and pulled out the banana muffin wrapped in a paper towel. "Did your aunt Sunny make these?" Marigold nodded. "Lovely! Now let's get cracking."

Marigold could just feel that this was going to increase her chances of being named Eliza Pruet.

"First on the list is the sand castle building competition. We need posters in all the hot spots: the casino, the library, and Edith's, to name a few. Art supplies are all in this closet. Oh, and we need someone to be the emcee, someone with a lot of flair and a loud voice." Immediately, Ashley came to mind. "Can I put you in charge of that?" Marigold nodded again, jotting down notes. "There will be an ice cream social before the regatta out here on the lawn, and I'm hoping you can help me with some decorations."

"I'm up for anything," Marigold said. "And I know Sirens and Sailors are playing after the regatta, but do we have anything planned for music during the ice cream social?"

"We don't! See? What would I do without you?" Jean asked.

"I'm sure I can come up with something great,"

Marigold said, feeling very *civic-minded*.

"You and your sisters always do," Jean said. "Okay, now I'd better going. I'd hate to offend the clambake committee. Maybe you can come with me on Saturday to meet with Edith about the ice cream social?"

"Of course!" Marigold said and then remembered her fun fourteenth. Her mood immediately dampened. "Actually, I won't be here on Saturday."

"That's right! You're going on a camping trip. How could I forget when it's all your aunt Sunny has been talking about?"

"Unless you needed me here to help you," Marigold said, brightening at the idea that she might have the perfect excuse to not go camping. "I'm sure Aunt Sunny would understand if it's for the tricentennial."

"I wouldn't dream of it," Jean said.

"Will Peter be able to sail today?" Marigold asked as Jean searched for something.

"Yes," Jean said. "Isn't it great? Mr. Rathbone will only be working inside today, so the docks and the lawn are ours—for now."

"That's wonderful," Marigold said, imagining how happy Peter would be to be able to practice for the regatta. She was relieved Mr. Rathbone's production schedule wasn't keeping Peter from his sailboat, not only because she wanted the best for Peter, but also because she was really hoping he'd still be her boyfriend this summer.

Jean seemed to be searching for something. "Are you looking for your sunglasses, by any chance?"

"Have you seen them?" Jean asked.

"They're on your head," Marigold answered with a smile.

"For heaven's sake," Jean said, and then she was out the door.

15 · The Boyfriend Test

Marigold decided the best place to make the posters was at the picnic bench by the docks. That was the spot where she was most likely to run into Peter, and she'd also be able to keep an eye out for Chloe. Marigold gathered the art supplies, left a note for Zinnie on the office door, and then made her way out the back entrance, passing several crew members carrying lighting equipment as she walked down the gently sloping lawn to the picnic table.

The morning sun was already hot, and a light film of sweat pricked Marigold's nose despite the breeze coming off the water. The water was a bright, sparkling blue, and it shimmered like tulle. She wondered if Peter was out on the water now or if he would be arriving later. Jean hadn't said. Before she could think any more about it she heard her sister calling her name.

Marigold turned to see Zinnie waving and practically skipping toward her.

"It's so weird to see all these trucks and stuff in the yacht club parking lot," Zinnie said as she sat at the table.

"I know," Marigold said.

"I wonder who they decided to cast as the waitress," Zinnie said.

"Me too," Marigold said, though she was a little thrown off that Zinnie thought she might have some competition. It's not like she was sure the part was hers, but she expected that her younger sister would be. "I guess they'll let us know soon. Anyway, our first assignment is to make posters for the sand castle building competition and hang them all over town. Here's the information we need to include." Marigold showed Zinnie the page in her notebook where she'd written down the date, time, and place of the contest. "Jean is worried that no one knows about it, so we need to make these posters really colorful and fun."

"Got it," Zinnie said.

As they each sketched out a design on their poster boards, Marigold noticed that Zinnie was grinning ear to ear.

"Who was that email from this morning?" she asked. "Was it Max?"

"Yup," Zinnie said, her smile growing.

"Do you want him to be your boyfriend?" Marigold asked.

"I don't know," Zinnie said. She focused very hard on her drawing.

"I think you do," Marigold said. "Your cheeks are pink."

"That's just because it's so hot," Zinnie said, shaking her head.

"Oh wow," Marigold said. "Your ears are like . . . neon."

"Well, now you're embarrassing me," Zinnie said.

"That means you really like him," Marigold said in a singsongy voice.

"It does not," Zinnie whined, trying to get Marigold off her case. "It just means I'm embarrassed by the idea of wanting a boyfriend, which I'm not even sure if I do."

"Here's the test," Marigold said. "If you get a bunch of emails, do you read the ones from him first?"

"Yes," Zinnie said.

"Do you spend at least five minutes a day wondering whether or not he's going to email or text you?" Marigold asked. "Those minutes can be all together or spread out."

"Five minutes? Hmmm." Zinnie thought for a moment. "Um, yeah. I think so."

"Okay," Marigold said. "And finally, on a scale of one to ten, one being not at all and ten being a huge amount, how much are you looking forward to seeing him in a week?"

Zinnie smiled. "Nine and a quarter."

"You like him like a boyfriend!" Marigold said, tossing her water bottle in the air and catching it with one hand. "You totally do."

"Whaaaat?" Zinnie said, waving her off. "I don't think that's a very accurate test." Zinnie turned and looked out at the harbor.

"Why do you say that?" Marigold asked.

"I'm looking forward to seeing Dad a huge amount, too," Zinnie said. "Like at least a nine and a quarter. Oh, look. It's Peter."

"Really?" Marigold asked, and turned to see Peter walking toward the docks. She waved to him, hoping that his mood would have lightened with the news he could practice all day today if he wanted.

"Uh oh," Zinnie said under her breath as Peter approached. "He looks mad."

"Hi, Peter," Marigold said sunnily. "We're making posters for the sand castle building competition. What's up?"

"What's up," Peter started, his voice threaded with distress, "is that these Hollywood people cast Vince as the dock boy."

"Who's Vince?" Marigold asked in a small, sympathetic voice.

"My skipper! The kid who's supposed to sail with

me during the regatta. Between Mr. Rathbone's production schedule and when Vince needs to be on set, whatever that means, I'm never going to be able to practice."

"I'm really sorry," Marigold said. "At least he'll be available on the day of the regatta, right?"

"When we'll lose because we haven't been able to practice the course," Peter said.

"Can you, um, practice with someone else?" Zinnie asked.

"I'm going to have to," Peter said as a cloud moved across the sky. "For now, I'm just going to go out on my own to clear my mind."

Marigold watched as he walked toward the dock with his head hung. Out of all the boys in Pruet, why had they chosen Peter's skipper to be the dock boy? She sighed. Handholding did not seem to be in her immediate future. But maybe she stood a chance of being his skipper?

16 · Best Friend Potential

Zinnie was putting the final touches on the fourth poster when she heard someone call her name. She turned to see Chloe, smiling as she walked toward her. Marigold had gone to hang the first three posters in the casino, the general store, and Edith's, leaving Zinnie to finish the last one, which she was instructed to put up outside the snack shack at the town beach.

"Hi," Chloe said. "What are you doing?"

"Making posters for the sand castle building contest," Zinnie said. Chloe was wearing jeans rolled up at the cuffs, loafers, an oversized T-shirt that said "Coffee, please," huge, vintage sunglasses, and a book tucked under her arm. Marigold would love this outfit.

"Cool, I'm just on a break," Chloe said, putting her sunglasses on her head so that they acted like a headband. "I liked your audition."

"Really?" Zinnie asked, feeling her cheeks flush.

"Seeing the same thing over and over can get really boring. But you were funny!"

"I was?" Zinnie said, hopeful that she may have somehow turned that audition around.

"Anyway," Chloe said. "I thought it would be fun to read by the water." She held up her book. It was *American Poetry: A Collection*. Zinnie couldn't believe her eyes. That was Mrs. Lee's favorite book. There was a tattered copy on her desk, and sometimes she read aloud from it.

"I love that book," Zinnie said. "I mean, I've actually never read it cover to cover, but it's my favorite teacher's favorite book, so I know that I'm going to love it when I do."

"I haven't read it either," Chloe said. "But my uncle thinks it's the best. He gave it to me for my birthday, see?" She opened the book to its first page, where Zinnie read *To Chloe, a young poet. With love from your uncle.* "And he knows I love to write poems."

"Cool," Zinnie said. She knew the power of a book, how it could feel like a door opening to a bigger world. "You know, I have a blog I'm writing for school right now," Zinnie said. "It's called *Coast-to-Coast Summer Adventures.* I'm comparing summer adventures on the East Coast to summer adventures on the West Coast."

"They are so different, huh?" Chloe said.

"Yeah," Zinnie said. "But my favorite thing to write is plays."

"Cool," Chloe said. "Right now I'm into poetry. Reading it and writing it. There's this one poet in here named Mary Oliver."

"I've heard of her," Zinnie said. Mrs. Lee had a quote of hers hanging in the classroom: "What are you going to do with your one wild and precious life?" Whenever Zinnie's eyes landed on it, she could feel the energy of the writer's question, which was a kind of challenge, and it thrilled her.

"I love her observations," Chloe said. "Did you know she used to live on Cape Cod?"

"No, I didn't," Zinnie said.

Zinnie had this feeling like she and Chloe had so much to talk about—that the whole world was going to be better understood once they discussed it.

"We should hang out sometime," Chloe said.

"Yeah, you should come over," Zinnie said. "My aunt has an amazing lighthouse."

"A lighthouse?" Chloe said. "I have a thing for lighthouses!"

"Then you have to check it out," Marigold said, appearing suddenly from behind them. "Actually, maybe you could come over today, after we finish making these signs, and we can talk about school next year. I heard that you can take two electives every trimester, and I have no idea what I'm going to choose. What's your concentration, by the way?"

"Dance," Chloe said.

"Awesome!" Marigold and Zinnie said at the same time.

"I have to work for my uncle later today, but I do really want to see this lighthouse," Chloe said. "Lighthouses are poetic."

Zinnie knew exactly what she meant. They *were* poetic: standing at the edge of the sea, watching for lost vessels as they beamed their lights across dark skies. She bet that Mary Oliver probably had at least one poem about lighthouses.

"Oh, um, do you know when they're going to let people know about casting?" Marigold asked Chloe.

"Oh yeah!" Zinnie said.

"I think sometime today," Chloe said.

"Do you know who they chose?" Zinnie asked.

"No, I don't get to go to those meetings," Chloe said. "Anyway, I can't wait to see the lighthouse!"

"How about you come over tomorrow at three," Marigold said. "I'd love to talk about high school."

"That sounds good," Chloe said. "I'll see you then." She walked down the dock, her backpack slung over one shoulder.

Unlike Marigold, Zinnie had never had one best friend. She'd always sort of been friends with every-one, but not particularly close with any of them. She understood now what it was like to meet a potential one. It was like when she was writing and having a hard time expressing what she wanted to, then thinking for a long time, and finally finding the perfect word.

17 · The Magic of Cake

"Anyone home?" Aunt Sunny called at the end of the day.

"I'm in here," Marigold called. She was curled up on the sofa with her iPad, researching Pinterest boards about ice cream socials and jotting down ideas. She was trying to keep her mind off two things. First, Peter. He had been so down today that she'd started to worry that maybe Mr. Rathbone's production really was going to ruin the regatta. Peter was the captain of the team and the best sailor in his class. What if he was too bummed out to lead his team to victory? It would be terrible if Pruet lost! And second, she was starting to get nervous that she'd been too cocky about getting the part in the TV episode. It was nearly five o'clock, and she hadn't heard a thing. Her dad always said that in Hollywood, good news comes in the morning and bad news comes in the afternoon. Here she sat, watching the shadows lengthen across the yard.

"Oh, good," Aunt Sunny called back. "Would you like some iced tea?"

"Yes, please," Marigold said.

Aunt Sunny walked into the room carrying two tall glasses of iced tea with lemon slices floating inside. As Aunt Sunny kissed her forehead, Marigold put her iPad down on the sofa and reached for the tea. Aunt Sunny had made it this morning. She'd poured boiling water over a whole bunch of tea bags and then added entire cup of sugar—the white kind, not the less-bad-for-you brown kind that her mother liked to buy from the organic section. Aunt Sunny had stirred it all up with a wooden spoon and then let the pitcher sit in the sun all day. She must've just brought it in and poured it over the ice, which crackled. The tea really did taste like sunshine.

Aunt Sunny took a good look at her niece and said, "Bad day?"

"Kind of," Marigold said. "I'm not sure yet."

"One second," Aunt Sunny said, and returned to the kitchen, emerging a minute later with a slice of pound cake heaped with fresh strawberries and sprinkled with confectioners' sugar. The sight of it made Marigold's mouth water, and when she tasted it, it was better than she imagined cake could be. It was buttery and spongy and absorbed exactly the right amount of strawberry flavor. And the strawberries added a brightness and tartness to each bite. "Oh my God, this is so good," Marigold said. "Thank you."

"I'd bring you a second piece, but we'll have dinner in an hour," Aunt Sunny said, turning her wrist over to look at her watch. "And I don't want to ruin your appetite. I've been to Gifford's Fish Store and picked up some scallops for dinner. Tony's getting some silver queen corn and peas from Goldie's farm stand, and maybe we can all go to Edith's for dessert. But first, why don't you tell me what's wrong."

"I really thought I was going to get the part of the waitress in Mr. Rathbone's TV show, but they didn't call me," she said.

Auny Sunny checked her watch and said, "The day's not over yet."

Marigold shrugged. The part in the TV show was feeling less likely by the minute, but maybe that would be a good thing. Then she and Peter could both be mad at the Hollywood people, as he called them. But she didn't *want* to be mad at Mr. Rathbone. She just wanted to get the job and be happy with him.

"Is there anything else going on?" Aunt Sunny asked. Marigold hesitated. "Does it have to do with Peter?"

Marigold nodded. "How did you know?" she asked.

"I had a feeling," Aunt Sunny said, putting an arm around her. Marigold leaned against her. "It was something about the way you were looking at him last night. You had stars in your eyes. And some hurt, too."

"I really like him," Marigold said. It felt good to just admit it.

"I know, and I think he likes you, too," Aunt Sunny said.

"He held my hand the other day," Marigold said, smiling as she remembered the feeling.

"How winsome and romantic," Aunt Sunny said.

"It was," Marigold said, snuggling against her aunt. She wasn't sure about the definition of "winsome," but she understood what Aunt Sunny meant. "But ever since we learned about Mr. Rathbone using the yacht club, it's like he doesn't even see me anymore." Having finally put the right words to her feelings, Marigold found herself on the verge of tears. "I've been looking forward to seeing him all year."

"That must be very disappointing," Aunt Sunny said. Marigold nodded again. She was *so disappointed*. "Peter has been anticipating the regatta all year, and I imagine he's so frustrated that he can barely see past it. It's like he's wearing frustration goggles."

"I keep trying to help him see the bright side," Marigold said.

"He'll come around soon," Aunt Sunny said. "Once

he gets a few good days out on the water, he'll cheer up. In the meantime, all you can do is be your wonderful, positive self. I know what will make you feel better."

"Another piece of cake?" she said.

"Yes, cake can be magic. But there's also something else," Aunt Sunny said as she stood up.

They went into the kitchen, and Aunt Sunny spread a map out on the table. "I found this over at the historical society today as we prepared for the tricentennial. They were going to throw it away, but I rescued it."

"I love the way the letters look," Marigold said, noting the vintage font.

"Isn't it lovely? But this is what I wanted to show you in particular." Aunt Sunny placed her finger on the map. "This is where we'll be canoeing for your fun fourteenth. And here is where we'll be camping."

"Great," Marigold said, but she felt her stomach drop. Her fun fourteenth was coming up faster than she wanted it to.

The screen door opened, and Zinnie and Lily came inside with their hands full of flowers.

"Aunt Sunny, we picked you a bouquet," Lily said.

"Aren't they lovely," Aunt Sunny said.

"We thought they'd look nice on the table," Zinnie said.

"We should put them in water," Marigold said. Just then the phone rang.

This, she knew, could be the phone call she'd been waiting for. A huge smile spread across Marigold's lips as she said, "I'll get it."

18 · The Happiness Pie

I t was a crazy thought, and Zinnie knew it. And yet she couldn't stop thinking about how she might actually stand a chance of being cast in Mr. Rathbone's TV episode. She'd genuinely made Meg, Mr. Rathbone, and Chloe laugh. And then when she'd run into Chloe at the yacht club today, she'd complimented her audition.

In fact, ever since she'd had that conversation with Chloe, Zinnie had been taking whatever chances she could to perfect her Massachusetts accent so she'd be ready in case they hired her. She'd even practiced with Lily in the pear orchard. About every third time, Lily said, "Okay, *that* one sounded good."

She was still holding out hope that evening when the phone rang in Aunt Sunny's house. Zinnie just about dropped the mason jar she was putting flowers into to race to the phone, but Marigold said, "I'll get it," and beat her to it.

"Hello?" Marigold said into the phone.

Zinnie put the flowers on the table and then crossed her fingers and put them behind her back, not wanting Marigold to see how badly she wanted this. A day on the set was sure to make an awesome blog entry—and she could even write about how unexpected it was to have a TV shoot in a sleepy East Coast beach town.

Aunt Sunny put a hand on her hip and leaned back a little, which Zinnie noticed she did when she was listening very closely.

"This is Marigold," her sister said as she pressed the phone against her ear. Zinnie watched as an enormous smile broke out across Marigold's face. She twisted the curly phone cord with one finger, nodding as she listened. "Yes, I can do that. Absolutely! This is great news!"

Marigold turned to give her aunt Sunny and her sisters a thumbs-up. Aunt Sunny raised her fists in triumph, and Lily started clapping. Zinnie smiled big, but inside she felt a familiar pang of jealousy.

It used to be a lot worse.

She used to want to be Marigold—to have the same hair and wear the same clothes and do all the same activities, especially acting. Since she'd discovered how much she loved writing, she'd become a lot more independent. Or had she? Because here she stood, feeling stung by envy. Why did Marigold always seem to get everything?

A moment later, after jotting down some details on the ancient pad of paper that was always by the phone, Marigold hung up and exclaimed breathlessly, "I got it! I got the part! I'm going to play the part of the waitress in Mr. Rathbone's TV episode!"

"Yay!" Lily exclaimed, and jumped up and down.

"Congratulations, my dear," Aunt Sunny said, and rushed to give her a hug.

"That's awesome!" Zinnie said, though her smile was starting to hurt.

"Well, your day certainly turned around quickly, didn't it?" Aunt Sunny said to Marigold.

"It did!" Marigold said. "Zinnie, can you believe I got it?"

"Yeah," Zinnie said. "We all knew you were going to. It's great." She'd gotten her hopes up, and now she couldn't help but feel crushed. "I'll be right back."

Zinnie dashed out into the yard and took several deep breaths. A moment later she felt a hand on her shoulder. It was Aunt Sunny.

"Will you come help me find those leftover sparklers from the wedding? It'll be fun to light them tonight," Aunt Sunny said. "I'd like to celebrate Marigold's success."

"Okay," Zinnie said. She really didn't feel like

looking for sparklers to celebrate Marigold, but it was hard to say no to Aunt Sunny.

"Thanks," Aunt Sunny said, putting an arm around her niece. "I think I put them in the garage after the wedding."

"Is that the canoe?" Zinnie asked when they arrived at the garage. She pointed to a boat literally hanging from the ceiling.

"It is indeed. Soon we'll take it up the riv-ah," Aunt Sunny said, and Zinnie smiled. She loved the way Aunt Sunny said "river."

"It's beautiful," said Zinnie, glancing up at the canoe's smooth underside. She couldn't help but notice some cobwebs. "Um, when was the last time you used it?"

"Twenty-five years ago, I think," Aunt Sunny said. "But don't worry. Tony is going to give it a once over and make sure it's safe for us."

"An old boat hanging from the ceiling, now a home for spiders but about to hit the water again soon. How . . . poetic," Zinnie said, thinking of the word Chloe had used to describe lighthouses. Zinnie loved this idea: that things, not just words, could be poetry.

"Aha! Here's that box of sparklers," Aunt Sunny said, holding up a container. "If it were a bear, it would have bitten me. Let's go back to the house."

After their dinner, Aunt Sunny, Tony, Zinnie, Marigold, and Lily stepped out into the dark pear orchard to light the sparklers. The grass was soft and cool beneath their bare feet, and the crickets were chirping a high, steady song. On the other side of the orchard some fireflies flashed. The sparklers hissed, crackled, and spit sparks. They looked like tiny fireworks and smelled of struck matches. Marigold spun in a circle, creating what looked like a Hula-Hoop of light. Zinnie wrote her name in the sky, as if her sparkler were a pen on fire. Lily leaped like a fairy, leaving a trail of stars behind her. Aunt Sunny and Tony held hands, their faces glowing in the light. As the sparklers burned out, they all cheered for Marigold—all except Zinnie, who smiled tightly. Despite the festive attitude, Zinnie was still having a hard time feeling happy for Marigold. She opened her mouth to congratulate her sister, which she knew she should do, but was so disappointed she couldn't find the words.

"I'm really excited that I'm finally going to be in a Philip Rathbone production. I have a feeling that this time it's going to work out," Marigold said.

"It's as though things have come full circle," Aunt Sunny said as she spread a blanket on the ground. Zinnie helped her lay the blanket flat, and then they all sat down and looked up at the stars.

"From what your aunt has told me, this is a dream come true," Tony said.

"That's right," Marigold said, pulling Lily onto her lap. "It is."

"I remember your first summer here, when you found out that Mr. Rathbone was in town and all you wanted was to be in that movie," Lily said. "It was the whole reason we put on that talent show."

Marigold nodded.

"The talent show was my idea," Zinnie said.

"And then last summer when you found out you'd been cut from *Night Sprites*, you were so sad," Lily said.

"I was," Marigold said.

"But you gathered your courage, and auditioned again, and look what's happened," Aunt Sunny said.

"It just goes to show that sticking to your vision pays off. In my day, they called that grit," Tony said.

"I've got grit!" Marigold said, and held up her fist like Rosie the Riveter in the poster that was hanging in her classroom.

"You all do," Aunt Sunny said, giving Zinnie's hand a squeeze, and then turning to her. "Zinnie, honey, would you like to go see the night-blooming jasmine?"

"Sure," Zinnie said, holding her aunt's hand. They walked to a quiet corner of the garden.

Aunt Sunny said, "Sometimes it's so difficult to remember this, but there's not a finite amount of happiness in the world."

"What do you mean?" Zinnie asked as Aunt Sunny

took a seat on the stone bench. Zinnie joined her.

"It can be easy to think that when one person has a moment of success, there's less happiness to go around."

"It feels like that right now," Zinnie said. "But I guess you could tell."

"It may feel that way, but it's not true. Goodness can actually multiply. It can be contagious. One person experiences goodness and then it rubs off on the next person."

"Really?" Zinnie asked. "How come it doesn't feel like that?"

"That's because when we feel disappointed at another's success, it blocks the goodness from spreading."

"But what if you can't help it? I mean, can you force yourself to feel happiness?" Zinnie asked.

"I don't think I'd put it like that," Aunt Sunny said. "It's more that if you can remind yourself that there's enough happiness for everyone, you find yourself sort of sliding into it."

Zinnie nodded, knowing that sometimes words felt right the moment they were spoken, and that other times they took some catching up to before they became real. It was like her dad's advice about talking to a tree. When he'd first told her to do it, it'd seemed ridiculous. But then later, when she had actually spoken to the great, leafy beech out of pure desperation, her father's instructions had felt as essential as the green grass beneath her feet. It was as though certain words were waiting ahead of her, farther down the timeline, to feel true. She hoped that was the case here. Because right now, it felt like happiness was a pie, and Marigold always got the bigger slice.

19 · A Moody Sailor & a Clueless Sister

"Mom, isn't it so exciting?" Marigold said into the phone the next morning. She couldn't wait to share the news about playing the waitress. It was only six in morning in Los Angeles, but she knew that her mom would be awake because she was an early riser. Marigold sat on the sofa in Aunt Sunny's living room, where the only phone in the house was. The morning light came through the window, placing Marigold in a rectangle of sunshine. Aunt Sunny and Tony had left for work, and Zinnie and Lily were waiting their turn to speak with their parents—or at least their mom. Their dad was almost certainly still sleeping. He was a night owl.

"It's incredible, honey," Mom said. "I'm so proud of you. Your dad and I are counting down the days until we get to see you again. This house is just too quiet without you."

"Oh, and I haven't even told you the best news yet," Marigold said.

"Better than a role in a TV show directed by Philip Rathbone?" Mom asked.

"Maybe they're equally as good," Marigold said. "I met the coolest girl ever here. She's actually Mr. Rathbone's niece. Her name is Chloe, and she's going to Performing Arts Magnet next year."

"That *is* awesome news," Mom said. "I wonder where she lives. Maybe we can carpool together?"

"That's the best idea ever, Mom," Marigold said, and already she could picture Chloe and her listening to playlists in the car together, comparing notes about classes, and discussing all the amazing projects they'd probably be collaborating on.

"It's my turn!" Lily said from the other side of the sofa.

"But leave some time for me," Zinnie said, pointing to the clock. "We need to have Lily at camp soon."

Marigold nodded. "Okay, Mom, Lily and Zinnie want to talk to you, too, so I'd better go! I love you."

"I love you, too, sweetie!" Mom said.

"Give Dad a hug for me," Marigold added, and then handed the phone to Lily.

As Marigold went into the kitchen to pack Lily's lunch, she realized that she had been unable to stop smiling since she'd received the phone call last night. Her other worries seemed to have shrunk as her happiness had grown. As she spread peanut butter on bread for Lily's sandwich, she wondered if the reverse was true, too. If she'd gotten bad news, would her worries and negative feelings about things have grown and her capacity for happiness shriveled? Maybe this is what had happened to Peter when he'd learned about Mr. Rathbone taking over the yacht club. His bad mood had taken over, keeping his feelings for Marigold out of sight. It wasn't that he didn't like her anymore, she realized with sweet relief. It was that he had, in a way, forgotten about the good things in his life. Like her.

Later, after Marigold and Zinnie had dropped Lily off at camp and discussed the plan for the day with Jean, they saw Chloe at the yacht club. They were on their way out, and she was on her way in.

"Going to help your uncle?" Marigold asked, then felt slightly foolish. Of course that was what she was doing.

"Yep," said Chloe. "Congratulations on your part!"

"Thanks," said Marigold.

"And sorry, Zinnie," Chloe said.

"It's okay," Zinnie said with a shrug.

"Sorry for what?" Marigold asked.

"I auditioned too, remember?" Zinnie said.

"Yeah, sorry," Marigold said. "Anyway, Chloe, I was talking to my mom this morning, and we were wondering where you live because we thought it might be fun to carpool over to PAM together."

"I think I'm taking the bus," Chloe said.

"There's a bus?" Marigold asked, but before Chloe had a chance to answer, Peter walked up, looking as grumpy as ever.

"Hi, Peter," Marigold said, recalling her revelation from this morning. She was determined to help him remember that there were a lot of positives in the world, even in the face of his disappointment.

"Are you going sailing now?" Marigold asked.

"Not here," Peter said. "I don't have access to the docks. I'm just looking for Mom. Then I have to try to find a new skipper."

"You know, I actually took six sailing lessons this year in California," Marigold said. "My instructor called me a natural."

"That's cool," Peter said.

"I'm just saying, if you needed someone to fill in . . . ," Marigold said.

Peter smiled, the first genuine smile she'd seen in days. "That's really nice of you. I'm not sure if that's enough experience, though. No offense. Most these kids have been sailing since they were five years old."

"Oh," Marigold said, her cheeks growing warm with embarrassment. She should've known that. Still,

Peter's smile hadn't yet faded.

"You must be a good sailor," Chloe said.

Peter nodded.

"He's an awesome sailor, actually. Oh, Peter, this is Chloe," Marigold said, introducing her friend. "And Chloe, this is Peter."

"You two haven't met yet?" Zinnie asked. Peter and Chloe both shook their heads. "Because she—"

"Really likes Pruet and she's our friend," Marigold said. She didn't want to reveal that Chloe was Mr. Rathbone's niece. The last thing she needed was for Peter to start talking about how much he didn't like the Hollywood people right now.

"I'm sailing with a buddy over in Omgansett today," Peter said.

"Cavorting with your rivals?" Zinnie asked.

"It's my only option," Peter said. "Since my parents rented out the yacht club to those—"

"I think that's great," Marigold said. Peter cocked an eyebrow. "Maybe you'll pick up some of their team strategies."

"I didn't think of that," Peter said. Marigold beamed. She was definitely lightening his bad mood.

"I bet it's going to be fun," Marigold said.

"I don't know, they think they're so great because their sail bags cost like two hundred bucks each," Peter said. "Why would anyone spend that much on a bag? All you do with a bag is put stuff in it!"

Chloe laughed. "That's so true!"

"Marigold once saved her allowance for a bag that cost—" Zinnie started, but Marigold interrupted.

"See you later, Peter," Marigold said.

"See ya," Peter said, and walked toward the club.

"I'd better get going, too," Chloe said.

"Hey, do you think your uncle might let me come and watch one of these days? It would be perfect for my blog," Zinnie said.

"Zinnie, I don't think—" Marigold started.

"It's fine," Chloe said. "You can hang out with me. We'll just stay out of his way. The trick is to be really quiet and just observe."

"Oh, I can do that. That's what writers do," Zinnie said.

Yeah right, thought Marigold. Zinnie may be a good writer, but her staying quiet and out of the way? Now *that* was unlikely.

20 · The Oldest House in Pruet

After Zinnie had helped Marigold convince Ashley to be the emcee of the sand castle building competition, which didn't take much since Ashley loved to speak in a loud voice and take charge of a crowd, Zinnie returned to Aunt Sunny's so that she could work on her blog. She was delighted when she saw that she had email with the subject "Pruet adventure." It was from someone named Brave13. "Follow River Road all the way to the end. Climb over the stone wall and walk through the pasture with the hay bales. Take a left. Check out the old house and then walk a hundred steps back into the woods. Climb."

What was she supposed to climb? A tree? It didn't matter. She would climb a mountain if that's what was waiting for her. Aunt Sunny's plan to spread the word about her blog had worked. Someone was helping her find adventure in Pruet! As she changed into her sneakers, applied sunscreen, and filled her water bottle, she wondered who Brave13 was. Maybe Ashley? She had told her about her blog in great detail. But Ashley wasn't the type to do something undercover. She'd just come out and say, "It's me!" She'd also told Chloe, but Chloe barely knew anything about Pruet. Then she remembered that Max had mentioned a mystery. Maybe this was it, or part of it anyway. Her heart pounded in her chest and a smile spread across her face.

She followed the directions that Brave13 had given her and sure enough she came to a house that was tiny and set back from the road. From where she stood she could see a plaque with words written on it. She felt a bit like Goldilocks, but she decided to walk up to the house and read the plaque, and it said:

This is the oldest house in Pruet. It was built in 1632 by James Pruet. He lived here with Eliza Pruet and their three children: Susannah, Patience, and Obadiah.

This had to be the old house that Brave13 was referring to. It really was an old house—1632 was so long ago it was hard to fathom. That was way before the United States was even a country. Zinnie wondered how this house was still standing. Did anyone live inside of it now? There were no cars nearby, but there was another plaque. It read: "Owned by the Pruet Historical Society. Open on Thursdays from 12–2 p.m."

Huh. It was some sort of museum. She took a selfie in front of the plaque, making sure the date 1632 was in the frame. Then she tucked her phone into her back pocket. Brave13's directions had instructed her to go past the house a hundred feet. She checked to see if anyone was around and then counted her steps aloud. She walked past some trees into a small clearing, and that's when she saw the tree with planks nailed into it for climbing. She looked up, and there was a tree house! It was small but enchanting, with a roof and a window and a little door. It was pretty high up there, too. This was without a doubt her destination! She snapped a few more pictures and then climbed. A bird squawked nearby. The wood was rough against her skin. She even scraped her knee on one of the planks, but it didn't stop her.

She was sweating when she hurled herself through the little door and into the small house. The infinity symbol was engraved on the inside. "Infinity," Zinnie said as she traced her finger along the sign. She leaned out the window, where there was an amazing view of the ocean. "Hello!" she called to no one in particular. She felt very much alone, but not at all lonely. Instead, the joy of discovery was running through her veins.

This is a place for something significant to happen, she wrote in her notebook. *Just being here makes me feel important somehow. How could a place like this exist without it being crowded with people who wanted to use it? Had Aunt Sunny ever been here? Had Peter? Whose tree house was this? Was it Max's? Who built it? Tony? When? Did it even matter?* Zinnie decided that it didn't. A place as beautiful as this belonged to the whole world. The question was, should she tell the world about it or keep it between herself and Max? If she blogged about it, would that ruin it?

After writing her thoughts down, she descended the ladder, which was a lot scarier than climbing up it, and made her way back to Aunt Sunny's. As she walked, she decided that she had to write about the tree house. She couldn't keep it inside. She scrolled though the pictures she'd taken, and they were just too awesome to keep to herself.

When she got back to Aunt Sunny's, she was thirsty and eager to get to work. She gulped down a glass of lemonade and brought her laptop to her spot in the backyard. Tony was by the garage, wiping down the canoe.

"Hey, Tony," Zinnie said as she sat down at the picnic bench.

"Hi there, Zinnie. You girls are going to have an awful lot of fun in this canoe," he said. "It's all cleaned up and ready for the trip."

"I can't wait," Zinnie said, and powered up her laptop. "Do you know anything about a secret tree house?"

"You mean the one by the oldest house?" Tony asked.

"Yeah," Zinnie said.

"Of course I do. I built it with my friends back when I was your age. Gosh, is that thing still standing? How'd you find out about it?"

"Someone sent me an email about it because of my blog," Zinnie said. "I think it was Max."

"I think it was too," Tony said. "He must really like you."

"Why is that?" Zinnie asked, brightening.

"It's the year-rounders' secret," Tony said. "People don't know where it is. It's only for the locals."

"Oh. Should I not write about it for my blog?" Zinnie asked.

"I think it'd make a great blog post. Just don't tell anyone where it is," Tony said with a wink.

"Good idea." Something about what Tony was doing didn't quite make sense. Then she put her finger on it. "Wait a second," Zinnie said. "You told me last year that you don't know how to fix up boats."

"I didn't," Tony said. "Until your aunt told me about

her plans to take you out in this lovely canoe for the fun fourteenth. That's when I decided I needed to learn, so I did a lot of research and asked some experts around town. And sure enough, I figured it out. Don't worry, now. I'll be testing it out for you."

"I'm not worried," Zinnie said. "My future depends on having adventures."

21 · Spirits in the Lighthouse

"And this is where the lighthouse keeper used to sleep," Marigold said, taking Chloe up the spiral staircase to a tiny bedroom, with a big round window, at the top of the lighthouse. It had nothing but a double bed, a woven rug, and a little dresser in it.

Aunt Sunny didn't feel comfortable with the girls sleeping here by themselves, but it was where their parents were going to stay when they came to visit. Personally, Marigold thought it would be a little spooky to stay here. The wind made the floors creak, and if she was very quiet, it sounded like the walls were whispering. She preferred to be out on the deck in the open air, especially since she had yet to try the diving board!

As they walked up the stairs, Chloe was light on her feet in her ballet flats. She seemed almost fairylike in her movements. *I should learn how to be that graceful,* Marigold thought. *I should definitely take some dance classes at PAM next year. Maybe I can even take some classes with Chloe.* Marigold also loved what Chloe was wearing today: rolled-up boyfriend jeans, a black tank top, and a choker necklace with a red rose in the middle of it. Zinnie, clomping in her sneakers and humming something, was like an elephant behind Chloe. Sometimes it seemed like Zinnie's presence took up twice the space of everyone else's.

"This place is amazing," Chloe said, snapping pictures with her phone as they gathered in the small room. "Like something from a fairy tale."

"Or a poem," Zinnie said.

"So true," Chloe said, smiling at Zinnie, who beamed back.

Ugh, Marigold thought. Why did Zinnie have to insert herself into the conversation? Why couldn't she just give Marigold some space?

"People are free to hang out with whoever they want," Mom had said to Marigold earlier this year when she was having trouble with Pilar and the Cuties. "And if they don't want to hang out with you, that's their loss. But you just can't control what other people want, even if it hurts your feelings. Who wants to be friends with people who don't want to spend time with you anyway?"

"Not me," Marigold had said, feeling temporarily

empowered. But the truth was that even though Pilar had chosen the Cuties over her, she still wanted to hang out with her sometimes.

Zinnie just didn't seem to have these problems as much. Sure, there had been the girls who had bullied her about her Stuffels at the beginning of the school year, but Zinnie had taken it in stride. It didn't seem to have hurt her the same way that Pilar and the Cuties had hurt Marigold. They had been the main reason she'd wanted to go to PAM, even though that would mean venturing out into the unknown. So she couldn't believe her luck at meeting Chloe. If only Zinnie would step out of the way, maybe Chloe would see what a good friend Marigold was.

Marigold had said that morning that she was going to meet Chloe at the lighthouse after she finished helping Jean gather and coordinate decorating supplies for the ice cream social. When Zinnie announced that she was coming too, Marigold had very nicely explained that this was a high school gathering. But Zinnie just didn't get the hint. She'd said, "Eighth grade is close enough! What's the big deal?"

Aunt Sunny was at the kitchen sink, washing the breakfast dishes as Marigold swept the floor and Zinnie wiped down the table. Lily was upstairs getting dressed. Aunt Sunny wasn't intervening, but Marigold knew that very little escaped her aunt's attention. *I will not fight with my sister,* Marigold reminded herself.

"But then who's going to take care of Lily?" Marigold asked.

"She can come too," Zinnie said.

"Or you can bring her to my office," Aunt Sunny said. "I'm going out into the field today to check on the plover habitats, and I think Lily would love to come. Maybe you would too, Zinnie?"

"Thanks, Aunt Sunny," Zinnie said. "But I think I'd rather go to the lighthouse."

"That's perfectly understandable," Aunt Sunny said, drying her hands on a dish towel. "I'm going to go check on your sister."

Marigold had been hoping that Zinnie would find something else to do this afternoon—like one of her adventures—but nope. Here she was.

"Yeah," Marigold said. "It's pretty cool."

"Pretty cool?" Chloe said as she took in the tiny room with its view of the sea. "It's the coolest place ever. Do you know when it was built?"

"Um, I'm not sure," Marigold said. She stood in the doorway as Chloe took a few more pictures.

"It was 1875," Zinnie said and flopped on the bed.

"Wow, this place is ancient," Chloe said. "It's seen so much."

"Wait, how do you know that's when it was built, Zinnie?" Marigold asked.

"Tony has a whole binder about this place," Zinnie

said as Chloe sat next to her on the bed. "I'll show it to you if you want, Chloe. It has diagrams and old logs from the keepers."

"Whoa! Yeah, I definitely want to check it out," Chloe said, hopping up from the bed to take pictures. "I love stuff like this. You could totally set a movie right here."

Marigold thought the lighthouse was cool, but she was more interested in talking about Performing Arts Magnet.

"Do you know which electives you're going to take?" Marigold asked Chloe.

"I'm not sure yet," Chloe said, looking around the circular room. "I think I'll just decide when I get there."

"Oh," Marigold said. She couldn't believe Chloe wasn't more excited about PAM. From what Marigold had heard, it was the coolest high school in Los Angeles. "I'm so excited for my shoot tomorrow!"

"Totally," Chloe said.

Marigold sat at the foot of the bed and tried to think of a good question to get Chloe's interest and attention. What was it like to be a famous director's niece? How was filming going? Did she ever want a part in her uncle's films? Were her parents in the film industry too? But before she decided on the right one, Zinnie jumped in.

"The local legend is that this place is haunted," Zinnie said.

"Wait, what?" Chloe asked, taking out her notebook.

"Everyone knows that's not true, though," Marigold said, hoping to lead the way back downstairs. This room was small and cramped, and she had set out lemonade, cookies, and a stack of fresh towels on the front porch. "Tony spent so much time here when he was fixing this place up, and he swears up and down that he didn't so much as hear a strange noise. So don't worry, Chloe, it's not haunted."

"Tell that to Ashley," Zinnie said, turning to Chloe. "My friend claims to have a sixth sense. She says this place has vibes."

"I think your friend is right," Chloe said.

"Chloe, you have to understand, Ashley is a little dramatic," Marigold said. "Come on, let's go back downstairs. We need to try the diving board."

"Wait a second, Marigold. Chloe, do you feel vibes?" Zinnie asked very seriously.

"I think so," Chloe said, and pulled her knees into her chest and closed her eyes.

"You feel a presence?" Zinnie asked.

"Zinnie, you always say you don't believe in ghosts," Marigold said. "Obviously, there's not a presence or Tony would have said something."

"Actually, yes," Chloe said, opening her eyes. "At

least I think I do."

"Oh!" Zinnie said, shivered with delight. "That's crazy."

"Next time I'll bring my Ouija board," Chloe said.

"You have one of those?" Marigold asked.

"My mother is kind of obsessed with this stuff," Chloe said. "And she's taught me a little."

"Do you communicate with spirits?" Zinnie asked.

"Nadia always says that her Ouija board and tarot cards are more about being open to our higher selves, not about, like, talking with ghosts," Chloe said.

"Wait, who's Nadia?" Marigold asked.

"My mother," Chloe said.

"You call her Nadia?" Zinnie asked.

"She says we're equals," Chloe said.

That's so weird, Marigold thought.

"That's so cool," Zinnie said. "I'm going to start calling Mom 'Gwen.'"

"Good luck with that!" Marigold said, laughing at the thought. But no one laughed with her. Did Zinnie really think it was "cool," or was she just swept up in the moment?

"I have an idea," Chloe said. "Zinnie should come to the set tomorrow, too."

"No!" Marigold said. She was looking forward to seeing Chloe without Zinnie around. By the look of confusion on Chloe's face, Marigold could tell she'd reacted too strongly. "I mean, Zinnie has so much work to do for her blog."

"No, it's perfect," Zinnie said. "I'm going to write about it for my blog—remember? I already asked Chloe about that."

"I don't know why I didn't think of it until now," Chloe said. "It'll be perfect."

Yeah, thought Marigold. *Perfectly horrible.*

22 · The Deal

"The canoe is ready for your fun fourteenth!" Tony announced to everyone that evening after dinner.

"Yay," Marigold said, trying once again to sound happy about it.

Aunt Sunny had just brought all the camping gear down from the attic and laid it out in the living room: the tent, the tarp, camping stove, canteens, and sleeping bags.

"That's a beauty of a stove," Tony said as Zinnie picked it up.

"Do you have fuel for this?" Zinnie asked as she examined it. Marigold put a pillow over her face and rolled her eyes. Zinnie's obsession with wilderness survival had started here in Pruet two years ago, when Lily had almost drowned. Of course that had scared the two of them senseless, and they'd enrolled in water safety classes as soon as they'd returned to L.A. Then last summer, when Zinnie had done the most amazing thing ever by saving Cameron, she'd decided she not only needed to be prepared for water emergencies, but also for those on land. So Zinnie had taken that camping trip in the Angeles National Forest, and now she thought she knew everything.

Marigold understood how and why this stuff was so important to Zinnie, but she was afraid that Zinnie was going to be a total know-it-all on this trip.

"I don't have any fuel in it yet," Aunt Sunny said. "But I'll make sure the tank is full before we leave."

"There's some fuel out in the garage," Tony said. "I'm very glad you're so well prepared, Zinnia."

"Marigold, is there anything special you'd like to eat on your fun fourteenth?" Aunt Sunny asked.

"As long as we can have s'mores, I'll be happy with anything," Marigold said, taking a deep breath and remembering the promise she and Zinnie had made that first night: no fighting. "Even hot dogs."

"Well, those we can roast over an open fire," Aunt Sunny said.

"You might even be able to leave the camping stove at home," Tony added.

"I definitely think it's going to be a fun trip," Zinnie said as she inspected the tent.

 149

"It will be heavenly," Aunt Sunny said. "Telling stories, sleeping under the stars— Oh, there's nothing like a little summer adventure with your sisters."

"I've never slept outside before," Lily said.

"Lily, with your love of nature, I might never be able to get you indoors again," Aunt Sunny said.

"And if anything goes wrong, I'll be able to keep us all safe," Zinnie said. "So don't worry, Lily."

"I'm not," Lily said.

"Aunt Sunny, did you know that Chloe, Mr. Rathbone's niece, is going to be going to Performing Arts Magnet in the fall with me?" Marigold said. "I feel like if she came on this trip, it would be a great chance to get to know her a little better."

"It would be so cool if Chloe could come," Zinnie said.

"That's not the tradition," Lily said, lying on top of one of the sleeping bags to test it out.

"There's something about camping with your family that's deeply bonding," Aunt Sunny said. "I really want you to experience it."

"Actually, Zinnie," Marigold said. "Is there any way you could let me have some alone time with Chloe?"

"Alone time?" Zinnie said as she carried a platter to the sink. When she returned to the living room she asked, "Why?"

"Because I feel like we have so much to talk about

 150

for next year," Marigold said. "But for some reason, when you're around—maybe because she doesn't want to be rude, I don't know—we never end up getting to chat about PAM."

"Wait a second here," Lily said. "Marigold, are you excluding Zinnie? No one likes to be excluded."

"Lily, I don't think this is really any of your business," Marigold said in her calmest voice.

Lily cocked an eyebrow. "Any sister business is my business."

"Zinnie," Marigold said, ignoring Lily. "I know she said you could come tomorrow to the set, but I think it's better if you didn't."

"Wait, what?" Zinnie said.

"Hey," Lily said. "Just because I'm the youngest doesn't mean my opinion doesn't count."

"You're being really bossy, Marigold," Zinnie said.

"I'm being a *leader*," Marigold corrected her.

"Hmph," Lily said.

"I'm going to make some coffee while you girls work this out," Aunt Sunny said, standing up.

"I'll join you," Tony said, and followed her out of the room.

"It's okay, Lily," Zinnie said. "It's just . . . I really want to go to the filming. She already said I could."

"You guys, we're fighting," Lily said in a loud whisper. "We have to stop."

"If you can just let me have some alone time with Chloe after the shoot, then I won't put up a fight about you watching my scene," Marigold said.

"Okay," Zinnie said. "You have a deal."

23 · Lights, Camera, Action!

Even though Marigold's scene was being shot in the afternoon, she'd needed to get to the set early to get into her costume and have her hair and makeup done. Zinnie had run a couple of errands for Jean, delivering piles of T-shirts that said "Pruet Tricentennial" to the general store in a wagon and typing up the itinerary for publication in the yacht club newsletter. She'd also looked at her classmates' blogs and checked her email about a hundred times, but there were no more emails from Brave13. *Or Max,* she thought with a grin. Right after lunch she headed straight to the yacht club.

She was sitting next to Chloe in the yacht club dining room, which Mr. Rathbone's crew had completely rearranged, though they had decided to keep the nautical flags that hung across the ceiling. Windows were blocked off with black paper, and the lights were huge, bright, and professional. There were at least fifteen different people working, operating cameras, checking lights, touching up makeup, and holding big microphones. And of course there was Mr. Rathbone, sitting in his director's chair, telling everyone what to do in a calm but firm voice. It was crazy to think that this was usually just the regular old yacht club, where the people of Pruet ate their hamburgers and lobster rolls after a sail and where Peter, who sometimes worked as a busboy, folded napkins and cleared the tables.

Zinnie actually got chills when Mr. Rathbone said, "Aaaaaaand . . . action!"

Zinnie held her breath as she watched Marigold emerge from the swinging doors of the kitchen carrying a tray with coffee, cream, and sugar on it. Even though she had been jealous of Marigold for getting to have the real adventure of the day by being in front of the camera, she was still impressed by her sister. She hadn't even said a word, and yet it was as though Marigold had been a waitress her whole life. In her yellow-and-white waitress's costume, which was nothing like the khakis and T-shirts the real servers at the yacht club wore, her hair up in a loose bun, and a professional smile on her lips, she definitely looked the part. She also resembled their mom more each day, especially with that makeup on. Zinnie wished her mom were here right now.

She watched as Marigold said her line, "Here's your coffee," and placed the coffee on the table like it was no big deal. She made acting look so effortless. Zinnie saw now how out of place her over-the-top accent must have seemed during auditions, even if it had been funny at the time.

Marigold walked back through the swinging kitchen doors, and Zinnie watched the scene play out. It was a conversation between a dashing man and a woman, who were plotting a jewel heist on a yacht. Someone off to the side gave a hand signal, and Ashley and a boy about Peter's age walked in the background, each holding a tray. Zinnie had to cover her mouth to keep from saying "Hey, Ashley!" She knew how excited Ashley was to have been cast as an extra.

Mr. Rathbone called, "Cut!"

"What did you think?" Chloe asked, turning to Zinnie.

Zinnie felt a little pinch in her stomach. She really wanted to stay in her director's chair and analyze the scene with Chloe, to hear why she thought it had gone well or poorly, and maybe talk about other scenes in other movies. She had a feeling they probably liked a lot of the same shows and stuff. But then she remembered her deal with Marigold.

"It was really cool," Zinnie said, hopping off her seat. She'd been surprised that Marigold had wanted to spend time with Chloe without her. But then she thought about how she'd asked Marigold to do the same thing with Max last year. Marigold had kept her word, so she had to, too.

"See, if I'd written the script, I would have made the dialogue even more lighthearted so that the poisoning would be an even bigger reveal," Chloe said.

"I love that idea," Zinnie said. "It would make the crime so unexpected." These were just the types of conversations she wanted to be having. They would make her a better writer. She regretted making the deal with Marigold.

"Did you see stuff you wanted to write about for your blog?"

"Weirdly, I was most interested in the extras," Zinnie said, thinking that it had been hard to take her eyes off Ashley as she walked around in the background, though she wasn't sure why.

"I know just what you mean," Chloe said.

"Hi!" Marigold said, approaching them.

"You were really good," Zinnie said.

"Thanks," Marigold said. "Chloe, do you want to go sailing with Peter and Vince and me tomorrow afternoon? It would be like a double date! Or do you have to help your uncle?"

"I'd love to go! I've never been sailing before," Chloe said. "Zinnie, are you coming?"

Before Zinnie could even think about saying yes,

Marigold gave her a quick but effective glare.

"I can't," Zinnie said.

"Why?" Chloe asked.

"The boat's too small," Marigold quipped.

"Can we find a bigger boat?" Chloe asked.

"Not exactly," Marigold said. "Peter, um, has only one boat."

"It's okay, because I need to write in my blog," Zinnie said.

"I get that," said Chloe, and then turned to Marigold. "Sure, I'd love to."

Marigold gave Zinnie a little thank-you nod, and Zinnie went to talk to Ashley, who was waving at her from across the room. Zinnie would have loved to talk more with Chloe, but she had to keep her promise. And anyway, now was a good opportunity to get the scoop from Ashley about the behind-the-scenes details.

"What are you, a report-ah now?" Ashley asked when Zinnie pressed her for specifics.

"In a way," Zinnie said.

"You put on talent shows, you rescue drowning children, now you're writing a blog. Zinnie, is there anything you can't do?" Ashley asked.

"Let's see . . . I can't say the line, 'Would you like a cup of coffee?' without making a total mess of it!" Zinnie said, and they both burst out laughing.

"Tell me about your audition again," Ashley said through her giggles. "It kills me every time."

"Here goes," Zinnie said, because she loved to tell a good story, and Ashley was the perfect audience.

24 · Not a Lie . . . Exactly

"How do you think that went?" Marigold asked Chloe now that Zinnie was safely on the other side of the room, granting her the space she'd asked for.

"It was great," Chloe said. "Trust me, if Uncle Phil didn't think it had gone well, he would've made everyone do it over until it did."

"I was so bummed out when your uncle cut my scene from his movie," Marigold said.

"That's not going to happen with this scene," Chloe said confidently.

"How do you know?" Marigold asked.

"Because in the script, the coffee that your character just served is laced with deadly poison," Chloe said with a smile.

"Really?" Marigold asked, suddenly concerned. "Does

my character know? Because I would have played it differently. . . ."

"Nope," Chloe said. "She's just an innocent waitress. But the male lead played by Daryl—you know the actor with the gray hair?" Marigold nodded. Of course she knew who Daryl Johnson was! He was *only* one of the most well-respected character actors on TV! "He barely survives this attempt on his life. The next scene is in the hospital. Which we're shooting back in L.A."

"So basically, if you don't show this scene, no one will understand the episode?" Marigold asked, grinning.

"Exactly," Chloe said.

"Yay!" Marigold said. Glancing over Chloe's shoulder, Marigold saw that Zinnie and Ashley were headed out the door, and she breathed a sigh of relief. "Hey, have you ever been in any of your uncle's productions? I love acting, so if I were you, I'd try to be in all of them."

Chloe shook her head. "Acting isn't really my thing. Nadia's an actress, and it's always just seemed so . . . I don't know. It's just not for me."

"Oh," Marigold said, feeling a ripple of uncertainty. Was acting uncool to Chloe? "Well, I guess I wouldn't want to do the same thing as my mom either."

"Really? What does she do?" Chloe asked.

"Film editing," Marigold said. "Kind of boring,

right? All that time just cutting and pasting."

"My uncle says that editors are the ones who really tell the story," Chloe said. "I was thinking of taking an editing class at PAM."

"Really? I want to take a directing class. Hey, do you want to go get some ice cream right now?" Marigold asked. "I know you said you're going to decide about electives later, but have you heard about the heroes and villains storytelling class? It's supposed to be awesome."

"I don't really have time today," Chloe said. "I'm working for Uncle Phil as a PA." Marigold nodded, impressed. She knew that "PA" meant "production assistant." It sounded so wonderfully professional. At the same time, she was disappointed. She'd been looking forward to having her alone time with Chloe. She guessed she should have thought about the fact that Chloe would probably be working. "But maybe we can talk about it tomorrow when we go sailing?"

"Yes!" Marigold said. "Tomorrow is going to be great. You'll see how fun it is. And Peter is one of the best sailors in Pruet."

"Cool," Chloe said. "I'll meet you out by the docks?"

"Perfect," Marigold said, and went to change out of her costume. She had almost reached the ladies' room when she realized something that would ensure their sailing trip went well. "Wait, Chloe," she said, hurrying back. "You might not want to mention that you're

Philip Rathbone's niece tomorrow."

"Why?" Chloe asked.

"Peter is the yacht club manager's son," Marigold explained. "And maybe you could tell this yesterday, but he's not exactly thrilled about, um, all of this. Especially not with the tricentennial regatta coming up."

"Got it," Chloe said. "That's fine with me. I like to go undercover."

"We don't have to lie," Marigold said. "But we don't have to talk about it, either."

Not mentioning something wasn't the same thing as a lie, was it? She took a deep breath and shook off her discomfort. A lie was purposefully telling someone false information. This was different. She was sure of it. Almost.

25 · The Quaker Graveyard

Later, under the beech tree at Aunt Sunny's, Zinnie wrote for an hour about what it had been like for a Hollywood crew to take over a small-town yacht club. She described the set, quoted Ashley throughout, and finished with a question for her readers: "If someone made a movie about your life, where would you want it to be set?" Then she typed the title of her post: "Hollywood Comes to Pruet." A moment later she saw that Max was online. A little flame sparked inside her chest.

She typed him a message.

Zinnie: Hi!
Max: Zinnie! Buena serra!
Zinnie: How are you? What's life like in Italy?
Max: this is the best food in the world!

Zinnie: Better than Aunt Sunny's?

Max: Well . . . close.

Zinnie: I went to the tree house.

Max: I know! I read your post. Awesome place, huh?

Zinnie: The best! Thanks for the tip.

Max: It wasn't me.

Zinnie remembered that the locals were sworn to keep the tree house a secret.

Zinnie: I know! I'm just saying it was so cool.

Max: Totally. See you soon!

Zinnie: Byyyyeeeee!

They signed off. How could a week feel so far away?

It was only ten minutes later, after proofreading and publishing her post, that she received an email from Brave13.

Have you ever seen a heart-shaped tree trunk? I know where one is, and it's a little bit cool and a little bit scary.

A link to a map followed the email.

A heart-shaped tree trunk? The flame in her chest burst into a conflagration. The word "conflagration" came to her in an instant. She had loved it when she heard a forest ranger use it once and had tucked it away in her mind for exactly this moment.

As Zinnie clicked on the link and zoomed in on the map, she saw that it was the location of a Quaker graveyard. A shiver went through her. Not only would a heart-shaped tree trunk make a cool visual for her blog, a graveyard definitely had the potential for adventure.

She really wanted to ask Chloe to go with her. She had a Ouija board! If there were any spirits in Pruet, they'd probably be in a graveyard—and communicating with them would definitely make a story. She could just picture summoning ghosts with Chloe and getting wonderfully freaked out, like she did with her dad while watching suspenseful movies. Zinnie loved the idea of ghosts, but she wasn't really and truly scared of them. What was more exciting was that the graveyard was probably bursting with poetry. Poems were likely hiding behind headstones and under rocks and in blades of grass.

Ugh! Why had she made that deal with Marigold? Zinnie was frustrated, but she didn't want to wait a whole day. She memorized the directions, pulled out a bike from the garage, and made her way to the next adventure with the wind in her hair.

When she arrived at the Quaker graveyard about fifteen minutes later, it wasn't nearly as creepy as she thought it was going to be. Set behind the old Quaker meetinghouse, up on a hill, next to a pasture where horses were grazing, it was a very peaceful place. And Max had been right: there was a heart-shaped tree trunk right in the middle. It didn't just kind of look like a heart; it couldn't have been more perfect if it tried. Zinnie snapped a picture.

Even more amazing was that it was in between the gravestones of Remember Smith and Eli Martin. According to the inscriptions they died in the same year. As Zinnie studied the dates, she realized they were both only fourteen years old! *They must've been sweethearts,* Zinnie thought. Maybe a colonial version of Romeo and Juliet had played out right here in Pruet in the 1600s! And Max had wanted her to see it!

As her heart leaped in her chest, she couldn't believe that she was feeling so cheerful in a graveyard. But she was—in fact, she was downright delirious with happiness. So this is what all the love songs on the radio are about, she thought. This fluttery, buzzy, blooming feeling. She couldn't stop herself from skipping around, spinning in a circle until she collapsed by Remember's stone.

How was it possible that someone had actually been named Remember? She said it aloud, repeating it as she considered what it must've been like to be called that. As she did, she realized that the word had a very pleasing sound. It was one of those words that seemed to carry a feeling in its vocalization. Okay, inspiration was striking!

Zinnie pulled out her notebook and started jotting down the uncommon names she spotted: Verity, Amity, Theodosa. Azuba, Comfort, Phoebe. Barnabus. Obadiah. Absalom. Together they sounded like a poem. These were some of the best names Zinnie had ever heard, and jotting down a list of them conjured up a cast of characters she was eager to write about later. She headed back to Aunt Sunny's, where she wrote her post right away. Two posts in one day. She was definitely on a roll.

26 · Love and Friendship on the High Seas

"Okay, Jean, all the decorations for the ice cream social are ready," Marigold said when Jean entered the office after her meeting with the tricentennial parade committee. "Come on, Zinnie, let's show her what we made."

Marigold and Zinnie had spent the entire morning making banners for the ice cream social. They'd used brown butcher paper to create cones and bunched-up tissue paper as ice cream and then strung them together with twine. Now, she and Zinnie proudly displayed their work to Jean.

"They're charming!" Jean said. "We can hang some from the tent posts and others across the table. I knew you girls would come up with something creative—these are so much better than the boring old signs

Mack and I would have made. And I'm impressed by how well you two work together."

Marigold and Zinnie exchanged a tense glance—they *hadn't* been working well together. Especially after Jean had informed them that Vince was not going to be able to go sailing as planned because he was needed on set. Zinnie wanted to go sailing with Marigold, Peter, and Chloe, and now there was no excuse.

"Why?" Zinnie had said as she cut out paper ice cream cones. "Vince isn't coming anymore so there's room! Besides, I really need to write another adventure, and sailing is perfect. Come on, you know how important my blog is to me and how much I need adventures."

"Didn't you just have two adventures yesterday?" Marigold had asked, bunching up pastel-colored tissue paper. "You went to a graveyard, right?"

"But I need to have eight before we leave, and I only have four so far," Zinnie said, dropping the scissors and shaking out her hand. "And my hand is hurting from all this cutting."

"We can trade," Marigold said, taking the scissors and handing Zinnie the tissue paper. "But you can't come sailing with us. It's high schoolers only."

"Really?" Zinnie asked, raising an eyebrow at her.

"I just want some space," Marigold said.

"Are we still on for today?" Chloe asked, peeking her head into the little office.

"Yes!" Marigold said.

"Are you okay, Zinnie?" Chloe asked. "You look . . . mad."

"She needs to come up with an adventure for her blog," Marigold said, answering before Zinnie had another chance to plead her case.

"I read your last post," Chloe said. "That graveyard sounded so cool."

"It was," Zinnie said.

"All right, so I'll see you out by the docks after lunch?" Marigold said.

"Yes," Chloe said. "I'd better get back to work. See you then." She waved and left.

"Girls, these are just beautiful!" Jean said now.

"And I'm not done yet," Marigold said. "I'm also going to make some bigger ice cream cones out of paper lanterns that we can hang from the tent."

"It's time for a well-deserved break," Jean said. "I know you and Peter are going out for a sail this afternoon, Marigold. Zinnie, what are you up to?"

"Do you mind if I check my email?" Zinnie asked.

"Be my guest," Jean said. Marigold cleaned up some scraps of paper while Zinnie sat at the computer.

"Oh, I got another email about my blog," Zinnie said. "Something about a bison! I'm supposed to look a bison in the eye."

"Awesome," Marigold said, relieved that Zinnie was distracted.

"Do you know whereabouts I can find a bison around here, Jean?" Zinnie asked.

"I thought you'd never ask," Jean said with a laugh. "There's one out at Featherbrook Farm, just a bike ride away."

"Have fun, Zinnie," Marigold said. She was itching to get outside to see Peter.

"See you later," Jean said.

It was going to be a perfect afternoon, Marigold thought. The sun was shining and the breeze was moderate and steady. She knew from her sailing class that it was great sailing weather. Even better, there was no way Zinnie was going to intrude on her group date. But best of all, she was finally going to be with Peter in the place where he was happiest—in a boat. She hoped that not only were the conditions right for sailing, but that they were also good for romance.

"Hi!" Marigold said as she greeted Peter and Chloe. They were waiting for her right by the dinghy, which Marigold knew was the little rowboat that Peter would use to take them out into the harbor where his catboat was tied to a buoy. Her prediction had been right. Peter's mood was better.

"Hi," Peter said. He was smiling again!

"I've never been sailing before," Chloe said. "Thanks for inviting me."

 171

"You're going to love it," Marigold said. "Let's get going!"

Once they got into the catboat, they talked about the differences between middle school and high school, and Peter asked Chloe where she was staying during her visit to Pruet.

"Just out by Charlotte Point," she answered vaguely.

"Oh really? Which house?" Peter asked.

Before Chloe could answer, Marigold said, "I'd love to sail for a little bit."

"Sure," Peter said, and handed her the tiller and the lines. "It might be about time to tack. Can you handle it?"

"Yes," Marigold said confidently. Everything she'd learned in her sailing lessons back in California was coming back to her. "Ready about?" she called.

Peter said, "Ready."

She let out the sheet and said, "Hard-a-lee!" And turned the little boat into the wind.

Peter clapped. "Wicked good job!"

"It's so cool that you know how to sail," Chloe said.

"I took lessons in Redondo Beach," Marigold said. "Next year you can come with me."

"Maybe I will," Chloe said.

"That was a perfect tack," Peter said.

"You aren't still looking for a skipper, are you?" Marigold asked. Her success had filled her with confidence.

 172

"Vince is almost done with his role, and he thinks we can practice enough in the next week to make up for lost time," Peter said. "But if he's not up to it, I'm going to call you."

She and Peter locked eyes and smiled at each other in the way Marigold had been imagining since that first day back in Pruet. The sun warmed her cheeks, the salt air twisted her hair, and her heart was as full as the sail that carried them swiftly and smoothly across the bay.

27 · Friendly Chickens, a Gentle Bison, and an Attack Goose

After Marigold had left to go sailing, Zinnie and Lily hopped on the bicycles that had once belonged to Tony's daughters and then set off down a long road in the opposite direction of town and away from the ocean. She may have one rude sister, Zinnie thought, but she also had one nice one—Lily—so she was happy to be taking her along on her adventure.

Zinnie had been okay with Marigold asking for some alone time with Chloe after the shoot, but did she really need to exclude Zinnie from sailing? That seemed unfair and mean.

She tried to wipe her negative thoughts from her mind as she and Lily pedaled toward Featherbrook Farm in search of the bison.

The latest email from Brave13 had been a little

mysterious. All it had said was "Go look a bison in the eye." It left Zinnie to fill in the gaps, which was actually part of the fun. Jean had told her all about Featherbrook Farm and shown her where it was on a map.

"Is he a . . . working bison?" Zinnie had asked Jean. She knew so little about farming. Did people use bison to pull their plows or something?

"He's more of a . . . pet," Jean had said, which had made both of them laugh.

Featherbrook Farm was two and a half miles away and in a part of Pruet they had never been to before. They passed a few farms on their way, and Zinnie wondered if it was possible that more than one of these farms had a bison. That seemed unlikely. And what did it matter anyway? Brave13, who she couldn't stop picturing as Max, hadn't mentioned that it had to be a specific bison. The girls crossed a bridge that went over a wide brook, which reminded Zinnie that they were going on the fun fourteenth tomorrow. She and Marigold had managed to keep their promise so far. If they could just get through the camping trip, they'd probably be able to make it through their whole Pruet visit without fighting.

They knew they'd arrived at Featherbrook Farm because of the hand-painted welcome sign and an arrow pointing to a little dirt parking lot and what looked like a store. They stopped to chat with the chickens for a moment. Lily plopped right down in the grass to get on their level. There was a station wagon in the driveway, and in the distance someone rode on a tractor, but other than that there didn't seem to be anyone around.

"These are just the cutest chickens in the world!" Lily said as she sat on the soft grass near the coop.

"I guess this is what people mean when they say 'free range,'" Zinnie said.

"Hello?" Zinnie called a few moments later as they stepped into the little store. There were baked goods, homemade jam, fresh vegetables, and some farm supplies. Everything had a price on it, and there was a plaque that read "$2 to visit our animals." But no one was in the store, even though the doors were wide open. There was just a sealed box and a small hole cut out at the top, with the sign that said: "Please pay here."

"Can we get some strawberries?" Lily asked.

"I only have four dollars," Zinnie said. "We don't have enough."

"I'd rather meet a bison than have a strawberry," Lily said, and Zinnie stuffed her money into the slot.

"How are they going to know we paid?" Lily asked.

"I guess it's the honor system," Zinnie said, and took Lily's hand and followed the sign for the animals.

"What's an honor system?" Lily asked as they walked toward a barn.

"It means they trust us," Zinnie said.

"'Beware of the goose,'" Lily said, reading the sign that hung outside the barn aloud.

Zinnie wrinkled her nose as soon as she set foot inside. It was also empty.

"Nothing to see here," Lily said, disappointed.

"But plenty to smell," Zinnie added, and dragged Lily out another door.

"Maybe that's where the animals sleep when it gets cold," Lily said.

"Maybe," Zinnie said. "Ew!" As she stepped in something squishy, she was really glad that she'd decided to wear her sneakers instead of flip-flops. She dragged her shoe across the grass to get the stuff off.

Now that they were on the other side of the barn, they could see more of the farm. Ahead of them were rows of what looked like lettuce, and a couple of women in long sleeves and big sun hats were walking the rows. Zinnie waved to them. One of them waved back as though Zinnie belonged here.

"There are all the animals," Lily said, pointing to a large pasture at the top of a gentle slope. Sure enough, as they wandered up the hill, the girls encountered some wonderful animals. There was a family of peacocks, a couple of goats, and an enormous pig. In front of each animal's area was a sign with a little information about it. They were all fenced off, but certainly had plenty of room to roam around. Lily greeted them all like old friends. Zinnie took pictures as they walked along and learned about the animals. This was so different from any zoo or petting farm she'd been to—partly because the animals seemed so happy and at ease, and partly because there was hardly anyone else here. She had never been so almost-alone with so many animals before.

A little farther along there were a couple of horses, also behind a fence, though they could have definitely jumped it if they wanted to escape. As Zinnie looked around, she couldn't imagine what horse would want to run away from this place. She read about the horses. There was a mare and a stallion, Stella and George, and according to the sign they were very much in love. Zinnie smiled to herself, wondering if this was another secret message from Max.

"Zinnie, there's the bison!" Lily said, interrupting Zinnie's musings. Zinnie looked beyond another, bigger chicken coop to a fenceless pasture, where a regal bison grazed. He was, Zinnie thought, the most majestic creature she'd ever seen.

"You're supposed to go look him in the eye, right?" Lily asked.

"Yep," Zinnie said, and together they walked toward him. It was kind of crazy that he was the only animal who didn't have a fence around him. Her heart quickened in her chest as they walked closer. This was definitely an adventure. The owners of Featherbrook

Farm wouldn't just . . . leave a bison here if he was an attack bison, would they?

Lily stopped in her tracks.

"Aren't you coming?" Zinnie asked. It wasn't like her seven-year-old sister could save her from a bison, but she somehow felt stronger with Lily beside her.

"I'll come say hi once you've had a chance to meet him," Lily said.

Zinnie took two steps forward and then came back for Lily. "You're coming with me."

"Let's sing to him," Lily said. "So he knows how nice we are."

"Good idea," Zinnie said. Holding hands, the two of them approached the bison singing "Twinkle, Twinkle, Little Star." When they were about ten feet away, the bison lifted his head and looked at them.

"Hello?" Zinnie said, making eye contact. "Do you have a message for me?"

He stared back at her with the biggest, sweetest, brownest eyes Zinnie had ever seen. Zinnie felt something melt inside her as she realized this giant creature was nothing but love. Kind, gentle love! A monarch butterfly fluttered around his ears. Maybe the message was that she didn't have to be afraid of her very big feelings for Max.

"He's so sweet," Zinnie whispered.

"I really do wish I had a bison for a pet," Lily said,

tilting her head and leaning on Zinnie.

"Me too," Zinnie said.

Just then the bison grunted. Lily and Zinnie froze for a moment.

"I think he's just saying hi?" Lily said, stepping slowly backward.

He grunted again.

"Uh . . . let's get out of here," Zinnie said, and the two of them turned around and ran back to their bikes. The bison hadn't followed them, so they were laughing like crazy at how silly they were to be scared. "I loved that bison," Zinnie said as she got back on her bike.

"I really want to pet one of these chickens before we leave," Lily said. "Do you think there's one in that chicken house right there?"

"You could check," Zinnie suggested, glancing at the small structure that resembled a doghouse. Lily took a few steps toward it when a huge goose emerged, squawking and flapping its wings.

"Aaaaah!" Lily cried, running toward her bike again, the goose on her heels.

"Scram!" Zinnie shouted at the goose to distract it while she struggled to get a hold of her bike. Thinking quickly, she grabbed a stick and pointed at the angry goose. "Get out of here! Go on!"

"It's the attack goose!" Lily said as she caught her balance and started to ride.

The bird then turned its attention to Zinnie, nipping

at the bike as Zinnie pushed off the ground and pedaled furiously. The two sisters biked as fast as they could out of the driveway. By the time they reached the bridge, their fear had transformed into giddiness, but they kept riding—not even pausing for drinks of water—until they were back at Aunt Sunny's, where they were certain the attack goose would never darken the doorway.

28 · The Fun Fourteenth

"Okay, are you all ready?" Aunt Sunny asked the girls, opening the back of the station wagon. She placed her canvas duffel inside the car and pushed it to the side to make room for the girls' backpacks.

Having spent the morning packing for their overnight trip, they enjoyed a delicious lunch of roast beef sandwiches with a butter lettuce salad from Aunt Sunny's garden and fresh cherries for dessert. After they'd washed their dishes, the girls grabbed their backpacks and headed toward the car. While Tony strapped the canoe to the top of the station wagon, Lily climbed into the backseat. Zinnie and Marigold both went for the front.

"Shotgun!" Zinnie called, grabbing the door handle.

"It's my fun fourteenth," Marigold said, and Zinnie released her hand and backed away. Even though she was mad from having been excluded from the sailing trip, she reminded herself that this was Marigold's big day and she was going to have to let her sister have her way for the next twenty-four hours, especially if they wanted to keep their no-fighting promise. Zinnie climbed into the back with Lily.

"I hope it doesn't rain," Lily said, pointing to some clouds in the distance.

"Me too," Aunt Sunny said as she turned on the engine.

"Let me put this in the back for you," Zinnie said, taking Lily's backpack and placing it in the wayback. It was heavy. "What's in here, Lily?"

"My bathing suit, a towel, clothes, a headlamp, jars for collecting insects and stuff, one of Aunt Sunny's microscopes, a scientific notebook, a magnifying glass, and bug repellant. Oh, and my toothbrush," Lily said proudly.

"You certainly won't starve," Tony said as he loaded the cooler.

"I brought hot dogs for tonight," Aunt Sunny said.

"And stuff for s'mores?" Zinnie asked.

"Would it even be a camping trip if we didn't have s'mores?" Aunt Sunny asked.

"Nope," Marigold said.

"I love s'mores!" Lily said.

"See you later, girls!" Tony said, and blew them a kiss. Aunt Sunny honked her horn, and they were off.

Aunt Sunny drove down the driveway, past the little town, and then took a left over a bridge they hadn't been on before, playing the girls old songs she had listened to with her sisters when they'd gone on their fun fourteenths. About ten minutes later, Aunt Sunny parked her car in a small parking lot near a beach with pebbles.

"This is the Pruet River," Aunt Sunny said, and they all climbed out of the car.

Those clouds in the distance didn't seem to be going anywhere, but the afternoon sun was warm. Together, they untied the canoe from the top of the car and lowered it into the water. They placed the cooler in the canoe and then loaded in the tent, sleeping bags, and the tarp. Aunt Sunny walked right into the water with her sport sandals and then helped the girls get into the canoe safely.

After a brief lesson from Aunt Sunny (even though Zinnie already knew all about canoeing), they paddled up the river toward Kettle Island, named so because it was shaped a little like a teakettle. Aunt Sunny told them they were going to sleep in the very same place where she and her sisters had stargazed so many years before.

The river was quiet and peaceful. The only people they passed were a few kayakers.

"I didn't even know about this river," Zinnie said. She was learning so many new things about Pruet on this vacation. It was amazing how many treasures this tiny place contained.

Aunt Sunny taught them some camp songs, which the sisters sang hopelessly off-key, and when they arrived at Kettle Island an hour later, they paddled close to the shore. Aunt Sunny climbed out and guided the canoe onto the beach. Zinnie directed them to set up camp right away, which was what she'd learned in her wilderness safety camp.

"But I want to swim in the river," Marigold said.

"Camp needs to be the priority," Zinnie said. "Especially if Lily turns out to be right about the rain."

"Zinnie, you're really thinking ahead," Aunt Sunny said. "And you're right. It's a lot harder to pitch a tent in the rain."

"Fine," Marigold said with a huff. "Tell me what to do."

"First things first, we lay the tarp," Zinnie said.

As soon as the tent was up and the stakes were in the ground to Zinnie's satisfaction, they changed into their suits and went for a swim. Swimming in a river was so different from a dip in the ocean. The water was softer and felt clean and brisk. They splashed and played until Aunt Sunny said it was time to prepare for the festivities.

"We need to gather some firewood," Aunt Sunny said.

"I can do that," Zinnie said. "Since I know what

kind of wood will burn the best."

"Very well," Aunt Sunny said. "Someone else needs to collect wildflowers. Enough to weave a crown."

"I want that to be my job!" Lily said.

"Perfect," Aunt Sunny said. "Off you go. Marigold, you can find sticks that we can roast our marshmallows on."

"Got it," Marigold said.

"I'll get some stones for skipping," Aunt Sunny said, heading toward the river. "Then we'll meet back here by the tent."

"They have to be green sticks," Zinnie said to Marigold. "Otherwise, they'll just burn."

"Thanks for the tip," Marigold said. Zinnie could feel the tension growing between them. *Don't fight,* she reminded herself, and went in search of dry wood.

Once they had gathered their supplies and Aunt Sunny had created a crown of wildflowers, Zinnie built a campfire and Aunt Sunny struck a match to light it.

"The tradition," Aunt Sunny began as they sat around the fire, "is that we take a moment to honor Marigold's childhood—all the qualities she's exhibited to bring her to this point. Then we place a ring of flowers on her head to celebrate who she is right now. And after that we'll each throw a stone into the river with a wish for her young adulthood."

"I'm not an adult yet," Marigold said. "I don't think I'm ready for that."

"But isn't that why you don't want me hanging out with you anymore?" Zinnie asked. "Because I'm not old enough? I'm not in high school?"

"Wait," Lily said. "Are you guys fighting?"

"No," Marigold said to Lily. "And, Zinnie, I'm just trying to make a friend at the school where I don't know anyone."

Aunt Sunny said nothing, though she listened to them thoughtfully. Zinnie reminded herself yet again that she had promised not to fight.

"We supposed to be honoring Marigold, Zinnie!" Lily said, her eyes wide with warning. "How about you say something that you love about Marigold first."

"Good idea," Zinnie said, and took a breath. "Marigold is a very talented actress. And I'm proud of her going to Performing Arts Magnet."

"I'm proud of her for sticking to her dreams, even when the going gets tough," Aunt Sunny said. "And I'd also like to say, I love how much she cares for those around her. She did a terrific job at my wedding last year, making sure that everything was just perfect for me."

"I love that Marigold is a good big sister," Lily said. "She always makes sure I'm wearing sunscreen and that I don't forget my lunch."

"Thank you," Marigold said as Aunt Sunny placed the crown of flowers on her head. "This feels pretty nice, actually!"

"As it should," Aunt Sunny said, and gave Marigold a hug. Then she handed each sister a smooth, flat stone. "Now we'll go down to the river and make a wish for Marigold's future."

They all walked to the river's edge.

"I wish that Marigold has fun at Performing Arts Magnet," Zinnie said, and skipped her stone across the flat surface of the water.

"I wish that Marigold marries Peter," Lily said, casting her stone into the river.

"And I wish that Marigold returns to Pruet year after year, always discovering a bit more of herself when she does," Aunt Sunny said, and pulled Marigold close to her. That's when they heard the voices.

"Look, someone's coming toward us!" Zinnie said. She peered out into the distance. "Another canoe with four people in it. And they're waving at us!"

Zinnie waved back.

"Oh my goodness," Aunt Sunny said.

"Who is it?" Marigold asked.

"I hope they're friendly," Lily said.

"I think they are," Aunt Sunny said. Zinnie saw the mischievous glint in Aunt Sunny's eyes.

"Wait a second. Is that Tony?" Zinnie asked.

"Yes," Aunt Sunny said, laughing. "It's Tony and some friends."

"Who?" Marigold asked.

"I thought about what you said, Marigold," Aunt

Sunny said. "About how traditions can grow and change. Your fun fourteenth should be just that—fun!"

"Really?" Marigold asked. Zinnie watched the approaching canoe and tried to make out who was inside. "Is that . . . Jean?"

"And Peter is with them too!" Lily said.

Even though Zinnie was happy to see Jean, Tony, and Peter, she'd kind of hoped it was people she'd never met before. Then she'd have another extraordinary adventure to write about for her blog. Maybe it would be a family of travelers, living off the land, with stories to tell.

"We brought extra chocolate bars!" Jean called.

"I thought this would be a good compromise," Aunt Sunny said as Tony and the others hopped out of the canoe and dragged it onto the shore. "If there's anything you girls have taught me, it's that I need to keep an open mind and let traditions evolve."

29 · The Not-So-Fun Fourteenth

*T**his is perfect,* Marigold said to herself as they all gathered around the campfire and roasted s'mores. She knew this was supposed to be a sisters-only trip, and she'd really enjoyed wearing the crown of flowers, but she was so, so happy to see Peter. Now it felt like a party.

The best part was that Peter was sitting next to her right now, and their knees were touching. Everything was falling into place. She'd finally had a chance to get to know Chloe on the sail—she knew Chloe would love it—and now it seemed like she and Peter were back on track for a kiss.

"Looks like the weather's going to hold up for us after all," Aunt Sunny said as the clouds parted and a big, round moon revealed itself and shone down upon the water. It looked like it was made of dented silver.

As soon as they'd arrived, Jean, Mack, and Peter set up their tent and Tony set up another one, which was for Aunt Sunny and him. "That way the sisters can hang out together!" Tony had said. "I have two daughters, and I know they used to love staying up all night and giggling."

Marigold smiled tightly. Zinnie had said nice things about her during the ceremony, but Marigold wasn't sure if she was just saying them for Aunt Sunny's sake or if she really meant them. Ever since she'd asked her for some time alone with Chloe, Zinnie had been distant. Marigold guessed that was what she had asked for—distance. And she'd gotten it. They were doing a good job not fighting. They were able to stop just short of it, but the one problem with not fighting was that the air stayed full of tension—even the clean, quiet air by the river.

"Happy birthday," Peter said. He removed the most perfectly toasted marshmallow from his stick and handed it to Marigold.

"Thanks," Marigold said, smiling. She had her graham crackers and chocolate ready for the marshmallow. When Peter smiled at her, she felt like her heart was part toasted marshmallow, sweet and gooey on the inside.

"You've gotten really good at sailing," Peter said as Marigold took a bite of the best s'more she'd ever had.

"I've been practicing," Marigold said.

"Peter has some good news," Jean said.

"Don't jinx us, Mom," Peter said, curving the bill of his baseball hat.

"Sorry," Jean said. "It's just that he's managed to sail quite a bit, despite Mr. Rathbone's production schedule and Vince's brush with Hollywood. . . ."

"And he and Vince made record time around the course today," Mack said.

"That's great," Marigold said. "I knew you could do it!"

"That's just me and Vince, though," Peter said. "The rest of the team has hardly sailed at all."

"Not everyone has your work ethic," Jean said.

"Shh!" Lily said. "I see a turtle."

"Where?" asked Marigold, knowing that keen observation was one of Lily's special talents. When it came to nature, she practically had an extra set of eyes. She was often able to see things that others didn't, like a grasshopper hidden among green weeds, or a worm burrowing into the earth, or a birds' nest tucked way into a branch. Apparently this was just as true for the nighttime as it was for the daytime.

"Look, right there," Lily said, pointing to what looked like a rock. "Do you see it, Aunt Sunny?"

"I do, my dear. Oh my goodness, I believe it's a diamondback terrapin," Aunt Sunny said as the rocklike creature moved.

Lily tiptoed over to investigate. She kept a distance from the little creature. Unlike other kids who rushed to touch animals, Lily seemed to be able to sense whether or not they wanted to be touched.

"I haven't seen a diamondback terrapin in years," Tony said.

"They are known to be very elusive creatures," Aunt Sunny said. "They were harvested into near extinction."

"What did people do with them?" Marigold asked.

"Turned them into soup," Tony said.

Lily gasped. "What? No! What kind of a monster would eat turtle soup?"

"Lots of folks," Tony said.

"It's such a shame," Jean said, shaking her head.

"I bet those Hollywood people would eat endangered turtle soup," Peter said.

"No they wouldn't," Lily said. "My parents make Hollywood movies, and they would never eat endangered turtle soup."

"Technically, they're threatened," Aunt Sunny said. "Though if we aren't vigilant, they'll soon become endangered."

"And Chloe wouldn't eat turtle soup either," Zinnie said. "She's a vegetarian."

Marigold held her breath, praying that Zinnie didn't say more. The last thing she needed was for Peter to know that Chloe was Mr. Rathbone's niece.

"Chloe? What's Chloe have to do with all this?" Peter asked.

"She's Mr. Rathbone's niece," Zinnie said.

"She is?" Peter asked, turning to Marigold, who felt herself blush.

"Wait, you didn't know that?" Zinnie asked.

Peter looked at Marigold with shock and confusion. "Why wouldn't you tell me that?"

"I didn't think you'd want to hang out with her if you knew, and she's my new friend, the only person I know going to my new high school—" Marigold started.

"Of course I wouldn't have wanted to hang out with her," Peter said, standing up. "She and her family almost ruined our chances of winning our own regatta."

"Peter, calm down," Jean said. "You and Vince are basically back on track—" But Peter stormed off. "He needs to cool down. Give him a moment." Jean cupped her hands around her mouth and shouted, "Don't go too far!"

As she watched him head down the riverbank with his flashlight, Marigold's throat was dry, and her heart actually ached. How could she explain to Peter how desperately she needed a friend next year, how scary it was for her to go to a new school, how horrible the Cuties had been to her, how sad she was about the loss of Pilar? Did boys go through the same things? It didn't seem like it. And what words did she have to communicate how much she liked him, how he made her feel as light as a butterfly, that she'd been looking forward to seeing him all year and didn't want to lose one minute of their time together over some silly details about where Chloe was from? And did he have any idea how stubborn he could be?

The thoughts were giving her both a headache and a sense of great urgency that she couldn't fight. She knew that Jean had told her she needed to let him cool off, but she had to talk to him right now. She grabbed her lantern, stood up, and walked after him.

"I'll be right back," she said to everyone, and fixed her eyes on the distant beam of his flashlight.

30 · Fires and Feelings

"I'm sorry," Marigold said as she approached Peter. He was sitting in the sand, staring out across the water. The river was lapping quietly at the shore, and the moon above was so bright they had shadows. "I didn't think it was a big deal."

"Not a big deal?" Peter said. He wouldn't look at Marigold. "I feel like an idiot. I feel like . . . you tricked me."

"Tricked you? No, no, no. I never meant to do that," she said, searching for how to say what she needed to, which was that she liked him, really liked him, and she just hadn't wanted to mess that up. It was that simple. But somehow telling him that felt way too scary. "Besides, it wasn't Chloe who rented out the yacht club, it was her uncle. She just happens to be here with him."

"Oh, come on, Marigold," Peter said, shaking his head. She winced at the way he'd just said her name like it was a bad word. "If you really thought it wasn't a big deal, you would have told me. Instead you lied."

"I didn't lie," Marigold said. "I just didn't tell you everything!"

"That's the same thing," Peter said.

"No, it's not," Marigold said, drawing back. He might've just been the most stubborn person Marigold had ever met. "Besides, what does it matter anyway? You were still able to practice enough, right?"

"Not the way we could have been," Peter said firmly. "Our team isn't ready for this regatta, and it's all that Rathbone guy's fault. If he hadn't shown up with all his people, we would've been just fine." Peter shook his head. "I can't believe I took that girl sailing. I can't believe she was in my boat. That's your fault."

"You know what?" Marigold said, her hands on her hips. "It's not my fault and it's not even Mr. Rathbone's fault. It's no one's fault. It's just the way things worked out. There were big storms here this winter, and the roof needed fixing, and so your parents were happy to let Mr. Rathbone shoot his TV episode—"

"Hold on," Peter said, finally making eye contact. "Are you saying this is my parents' fault because we didn't have enough money of our own to fix the roof?"

"What? No, that's crazy," Marigold said. "Peter,

 197

you're not even listening. Forget it!"

She turned around and headed back toward their camp, where everyone's faces were lit by the fire. She didn't want to see anyone, especially not Zinnie, but she wasn't about to hang around with Peter anymore, and she was scared to walk beyond him into the woods. Marigold stopped short of rejoining the group. She was stuck, so she stood still for a moment contemplating her next move while her heart thumped in her chest.

"Everything okay?" Aunt Sunny asked.

"Yes," Marigold said. Zinnie was looking at her, eyes round with concern. But Marigold didn't think she could get any closer to Zinnie without wanting to scream her head off—and they'd promised not to fight. Marigold took a deep breath and said as calmly as she could, "Peter just needs time, like Jean said. And I'm really tired, so I'm going to bed. Good night."

"Good night, love," Aunt Sunny said.

Marigold kicked off her sneakers, unzipped the tent, and crawled inside, pulling her sleeping bag around her. Her mind was racing, and though she wanted to cry, tears wouldn't come. Bits of conversation and laughter from around the campfire drifted her way like embers, which only made her feel more alone. She wrapped her sweatshirt around her head and tried to go to sleep.

31 · Adrift

Zinnie understood why Aunt Sunny loved this place so much. The river, which lapped gently against the shore, was such a peaceful place, especially now that Marigold had zipped herself in the tent. The night air was cool and crisp, and the fire warm and crackling. There was something about sitting around a campfire toasting marshmallows that seemed to draw everyone a few inches closer together. Lily was leaning against her, Jean and Mack were holding hands, and Tony poked at the fire with a long stick to keep it roaring. Aunt Sunny was telling the story of how Beatrice and Esther used to catch fish from the river for their fun fourteenth meal when Zinnie noticed something odd.

"Um, where's the other canoe?" Zinnie said. The canoe Tony and the Pasques had arrived in was now just . . . gone.

"Dear me," Aunt Sunny said, standing up. "She's right."

"We pulled it up on the beach," Jean said. "I did it myself."

"Not far enough," Mack said.

"I really don't think that's helpful, dear," Jean said.

"Neither of us has gone camping since college," Mack said.

"I see it!" Zinnie said. "It's drifted downstream— and it's capsized!"

"We flipped it over on the beach," Mack said. "We thought that would keep dry in case of rain."

"The river rose with the tide," Tony said.

"We need a plan," Zinnie said. Part of Zinnie's wilderness training had been out on a lake, and she knew all about how to climb back into an overturned canoe. But they had to move quickly since the canoe was drifting with the current.

"What do we do?" Lily asked.

"We're going to have to get it," Aunt Sunny said, though she didn't seem to have a solution.

Peter was now running up the shore. "The canoe's gone?" he asked.

"It's right there," Zinnie said, pointing. "Okay, this is what we need to do. Four of us need to take the canoe that's still here and catch up to it, and then Peter and I will jump in and turn it over. Oh, and we can't forget the other set of paddles."

"Mack and I will go with Peter and Zinnie—this is our fault, after all," Jean said. "You and Tony stay here with Lily and Marigold."

"If you say so," Aunt Sunny said. "Please be careful."

Peter quickly untied the remaining canoe, and as he and Mack pushed it into the water, Zinnie and Jean climbed inside. Tony passed them the extra paddles. As Jean and Mack paddled toward the drifting canoe, Zinnie noticed that Marigold had emerged from the tent and was watching from the shore.

"Go, Zinnie, go!" Lily called, cheering them on.

When they reached the capsized canoe, Zinnie gave instructions. "So, Peter, you and I will get in the water and swim under the canoe." Peter nodded, up for anything nautical, as usual. "And together, we'll lift it. Jean and Mack, we'll need you helping from inside this canoe, so that one side of that canoe can rest on this one—"

"Hopefully we all won't end up in the drink!" Mack said.

"As long as you two can stay balanced in there, it should work," Zinnie said. "So then the water will drain out and we can flip it over, and then Peter and I will have to climb inside of it."

"Sounds like a plan, Zinnie," Jean said.

"Ready, Peter?" Zinnie asked.

He smiled, took off his T-shirt, and they jumped

in. The water was cold and dark, but also soft and smooth compared to ocean water. Very carefully, they performed the maneuver to drain the canoe.

"Way to go, guys," Mack said as they all worked together to flip the canoe so it was upright again. "So now how do we get in without tipping it?" Peter asked.

"Okay," Zinnie said, remembering everything she'd learned. "We need to get on opposite sides, close to the center, but far enough away from each other so we don't collide. Then, on the count of three, we both lift our torsos inside. Okay?"

"Got it," Peter said. "Ready? One, two, three!"

Zinnie and Peter both hoisted themselves on the canoe. Peter started to throw a leg over, and the canoe started to rock.

"Wait," Zinnie said. "We need to go at the same time—but just one leg first!"

"All right," Peter said, and they both started to giggle for some reason. Zinnie counted. "One, two, three!"

They both put one leg into the canoe, and once again, broke into a laughing fit as the canoe rocked back and forth.

"What's so funny?" Mack asked from the other canoe.

"This!" Zinnie said, gesturing to their awkward positions. Her whole body was soaking wet and her hair no doubt frizzing beyond belief. Still, she couldn't help but see the humor in the situation.

"Same thing with the other leg?" Peter asked.

"Yup," Zinnie said. "One, two, three!"

Once again, the canoe rocked as she and Peter found their balance. Peter scrambled to the bow, and Zinnie gingerly stepped to the stern. They had done it! They had rescued the canoe!

Mack and Jean clapped. Zinnie heard everyone on shore cheering—except, she thought, Marigold.

"High five!" Peter said, offering his palm, and Zinnie obliged with a satisfying slap.

32 · Tent Talks

Marigold didn't wait for Jean, Mack, Peter, and Zinnie to arrive back at the shore. Instead, she slinked back into the tent.

Minutes later, she heard footsteps, and then Zinnie poked her head inside.

"That was fun," Zinnie said. She was soaking wet and dripping water everywhere. "Did you see that?"

"Yes, I did, Miss Show-Off," Marigold said. "Now can you get out of this tent before everything gets totally soaked?"

"Miss Show-Off? How about Miss Hero, and I need my clothes, which are inside the tent because in case you didn't notice, I'm totally sopping wet."

"Here," Marigold said, tossing Zinnie's bag outside the tent.

"Where am I supposed to change?" Zinnie asked.

"In the woods," Marigold said.

Zinnie stormed off somewhere out of sight to change, and then reappeared moments later.

"I really think you should find somewhere else to sleep tonight," Marigold said.

"What? I can't find somewhere else to sleep tonight," Zinnie said.

"You can sleep outside," Marigold said, gathering one of the other sleeping bags so she could throw it outside the tent.

"Except that it's starting to rain," Zinnie said, climbing back inside, her hair still a wet mop. Lily tumbled in after her. "What is your problem? Are you mad at me?"

"Yes! You weren't supposed to tell Peter that Chloe is Mr. Rathbone's niece," Marigold hissed as Zinnie used Marigold's sweatshirt to towel off her hair. "Oh! How dare you use my sweatshirt. Give it back!" Marigold said, ripping it from her sister's hands.

"You don't have to get violent!" Zinnie snapped.

"Would you two shush?" Lily said.

"Besides, I didn't know that Peter didn't know about Chloe," Zinnie said as the rain pitter-pattered on the tent walls.

"Shh," Lily said. "You don't want Aunt Sunny to hear you fighting."

"I mean, how was I supposed to know that?" Zinnie whispered.

"It's common sense," Marigold whispered back. "There's no way he's going to want to hang out with her now that she's one of the Hollywood people. And she's my only hope of starting school with a new friend. So now, thanks to you, I have to choose whether I want a boyfriend or a best friend."

"It was a simple mistake," Zinnie said. "It's your fault for telling a lie."

"It wasn't a lie," Marigold said, having now been over this in her head a hundred times. "It just wasn't the whole truth."

"Same thing," Zinnie said.

"You guys think you're whispering," Lily said harshly. "But you're not. This fun fourteenth means so much to Aunt Sunny, and she worked really hard to plan it. Do you want her to think it turned out badly just because you two couldn't get along?" Marigold and Zinnie shook their heads. "Okay, then. Do I have to remind you of the rule we learned in kindergarten? If you can't say anything nice, then don't say anything at all."

"Fine," Zinnie said, and rolled to one side of the tent.

"Fine," said Marigold, rolling to the other. Then she rolled back. "But did you have to go and have a fun rescue mission with Peter?"

"Yes!" Zinnie said. "The canoe was floating away!"

"I know that, Zinnie. I'm not dumb. But why did

you have to go with Peter—couldn't Aunt Sunny have gone?"

"I'm the one who knew what to do because of my wilderness weekend!" Zinnie said.

Marigold huffed. "If I have to hear one more word about your stupid wilderness weekend, I think I'm going to throw up."

"Excuse me?" Zinnie said. "That is so rude!"

"You guys are both rude!" Lily said. "And if you two speak one more word to each other tonight, I'm going to . . . Ugh. I don't know. I'm going to . . . pee in this tent!"

"Ew," Marigold and Zinnie said together. But then they finally shut up.

33 · A Sister Needs to Take Care of Herself, Right?

When Zinnie opened her laptop on Monday morning, she realized that her last blog post about the bison had been a huge hit. She'd added some really great pictures, including an action shot of the attack goose. She couldn't believe it, but there were twenty-three comments about the post! There was even one comment from Mrs. Lee. She'd written: "Your search for adventure is paying off. Just when I think you can't top your last one, you do! Way to go!" And of course there was a comment from Max: "Sounds awesome!" Zinnie smiled as she reread that comment a bunch of times. One of the pictures she'd posted was of the horses in love. She'd included it to send a little signal back to Max, one that said *I'm no-*

ticing all of these clues and I like you, too. Where, she wondered, would he lead her next?

Zinnie then got straight to work typing a story about the latest adventure—the fun fourteenth. She played up the part about rescuing the canoe, though the true adventure had been spending the night in a zipped-up tent next to a sister who was furious with her. After last summer's fiasco, she had promised not to write about Marigold ever again, though she regretted that promise now. Zinnie had no intention of libeling her sister; she just wanted to write about the actual story. *Oh well,* she sighed.

Zinnie was debating whether or not it was good enough to publish when Marigold marched outside and said, "I'm going to take Lily to camp, and then I'm going to help Jean. Are you coming?" They hadn't been fighting, but they'd also been far from friendly. Zinnie still felt like Marigold was being completely unfair, and Marigold was obviously not ready to forgive her for revealing her deception.

"I can't," Zinnie said. "I need to work on my blog."

"You've been working on it all morning," Marigold said. "And I need your help copying and folding the programs for the historical house tour. And we have to paint a sign for Aunt Sunny's exhibit on piping plovers. Zinnie, we don't have a lot of time. You really aren't a very good assistant."

"Because I'm not your assistant!" Zinnie said.

"Guys," Lily said. "It sounds like you're fighting again."

"We're not," Zinnie said. "It's just that I can't help with all of that. If I want to be editor in chief, I need to do my very best. I can't just do your bidding all the time."

"Okay," Marigold said in a calm voice, though Zinnie could tell from the tightness of her lips that she was doing everything she could not to yell at her.

Sometimes a sister has to take care of herself, Zinnie thought. She experienced a brief feeling of empowerment, but it was soon squashed by the sense that she was letting everybody down. How was a person supposed to know, she wondered, when to take care of herself and when to take care of others?

"Oh, and I saw this morning that one of your friends' blogs is being featured on Huzzah.com," Marigold said.

"What?" Zinnie asked. "The real Huzzah.com?"

"The supercool website that has everything the modern girl wants to know, from fashion to politics, yes. That one," Marigold said.

"Really?" Zinnie asked, deflated.

"Yeah, check it out," Marigold said.

"Bye, Zinnie," Lily said as she and Marigold walked down the driveway.

"Bye," Zinnie said, and immediately went to Huzzah. There it was. Madison Valenzuela's blog *Sea Change*! It had over a thousand shares! Zinnie put her head in her hands. Did she even stand a chance of being editor in chief? Was it worth trying? How could she compete with this? Regardless, she was going to have to complete the assignment, so she returned to her post and tried to make it better.

34 · The Whole Real Truth

Marigold had been anxious to see Peter again. They'd avoided each other the morning after the fun fourteenth, when Aunt Sunny had made them all oatmeal on the camp stove. Marigold could barely get a bite down, and Peter wouldn't meet her eyes. And then he, Mack, and Jean had taken off early. She'd been hoping to see him at the yacht club today when she was working for Jean, but that was one of the days that Mr. Rathbone was using the docks, so Peter hadn't been there. Marigold was both worried and relieved in the very same moment when she saw that Peter had decided to come along with Jean and join Aunt Sunny, Tony, Zinnie, and Lily for the "clean out your fridge" picnic on the beach.

This meant that everyone made something from the food in the refrigerator that needed to be eaten. The idea was to not let any food go to waste. It was best to choose a very scenic spot, Aunt Sunny had explained, in case the cooking wasn't top notch. So, of course they'd decided to go to the beach with the big dunes and a view of Martha's Vineyard in the far distance.

Ever since their first visit to Pruet, Marigold and her sisters had loved this beach. They had to drive down a long and winding country road to get here, through a pasture where hairy cows wandered free. There was a wide gate at the entrance, and Marigold, as the oldest child, was the one responsible for hopping out of the car and opening it so that they could drive through, and then closing it behind them once they had passed. The gate was to prevent the cows from escaping, though Marigold couldn't understand why anyone, person or animal, would want to escape this beautiful place.

And yet, a part of her did want to escape. This was partially because she had absolutely no desire to spend time with Zinnie after she'd spilled the beans about Chloe and then refused to help her with the tricentennial preparations. And also because her heart was beating so fast as she watched Peter and his parents come down the dune carrying the cooler, her instinct was to hide and not confront him. However, she'd made up her mind that day as she was painting tricentennial signs, that she needed to talk to him and explain why she hadn't told him about Chloe. She'd thought about it, almost to the exclusion of everything else, and realized that she had, in a way, tricked him, despite her innocent intentions. And maybe his mom had been right—he needed to cool down before he was capable of hearing her point of view.

As he approached she thought he was looking especially handsome in his Pruet sailing T-shirt. All that time out on the water had given his skin a glow that Marigold found irresistible.

"Peter," Marigold said before she had a chance to lose her courage. "I think we need to talk."

"Okay," Peter said with a nod.

As Aunt Sunny, Tony, Jean, Mack, and her sisters set out the picnic blanket and food, Marigold gestured for Peter to follow her down the beach. The breeze was warm, and the sun threaded the water with gold. Once they were out of earshot of the rest of the group, Marigold gathered herself and said, "I'm sorry that I didn't tell you who Chloe was right away." Peter nodded again, and she could tell that she had his full attention. "You were right in that, well, I thought you'd never want to hang out with her if you knew she was Mr. Rathbone's niece, so I didn't tell you."

"It made me feel like an idiot," Peter said.

"I'm sorry," Marigold said, and gave the words a few moments to land. "What you don't know is that I had a really rough year with friends in eighth grade."

"You did?" Peter said.

"Yeah," Marigold said. "I pretty much had no friends all year."

"That must have been hard," Peter said.

"It's why I decided to switch schools," Marigold said. She walked closer to the water so that when the waves rolled in, the foam would wash over her toes.

"I didn't know that," Peter said.

"So when I found out that Chloe was going to my new school, I just really wanted to get to know her better. And at the same time," she started, but felt a bit short of breath, "I also wanted to spend time with you. So that's, kind of, what happened."

"Makes more sense now," Peter said. "I still feel kind of weird about it, though."

"Okay," Marigold said. She hoped that Peter might say something about how he wanted to spend more time with her as well, but instead, he walked quietly next to her. Did his silence mean that he didn't like her anymore? She felt better about having told him the whole, real truth, but began to worry that she really had ruined her chance at having a boyfriend this summer. She decided to give him thirty more seconds to tell her that he was sorry about overreacting last night and that he wanted to spend more time with her, and after that she was going to end this walk. When he didn't say a word, she said, "Let's go eat. I'm getting hungry." And she turned around and raced back to the picnic with the wind at her back.

When they returned to the picnic, Jean was staring at her phone in horror.

"I knew it was too good to be true!" Jean said.

"What's wrong?" Aunt Sunny asked.

"Yeah, Mom," Peter said. "What happened?"

"It's Sirens and Sailors," Jean answered with a sigh. "They've booked a last-minute gig at an important venue in New York City and won't be able to perform at the tricentennial!"

"They abandoned ship?" Tony asked. Jean nodded. "That's too bad."

"But they already made a commitment to us!" Zinnie said, indignant.

"It was just a handshake deal," Mack said. "We didn't use contracts. Never in a million years did I think we'd have to. They're locals. It was only two years ago that their lead singer was teaching at our sailing school."

"They're locals who got famous," Peter said, shaking his head. "So now they're only thinking about themselves, just like those Hollywood people."

"Peter, enough with that," Jean said. "These dear girls are from Hollywood."

"Not all Hollywood people are bad," Lily said, scooping some potato salad onto her plate. "Like my mom and dad. They're the best."

"I know," Marigold said. "We can take the place of Sirens and Sailors. Zinnie will write something, I'll direct it, and we'll all perform it."

"You will?" Peter asked.

"Maybe we should think about this," Zinnie said. "It's not like we have a lot of time."

"We can do it!" Marigold said, taking in Zinnie's skeptical look. "We just need to work quickly."

"You're right about that," Aunt Sunny said.

"Zinnie, Lily, and I might be from California, but we love Pruet so much. Don't worry, Jean. We won't let you down."

"You girls *are* incredibly creative," Jean said.

"I don't know if we . . . ," Zinnie started.

"Don't you love Pruet?" Marigold said.

"Of course," Zinnie said.

"Then it's settled," Marigold said.

There was no way Peter would think of her as just a summer person now. And this would definitely put her in the running to be Eliza Pruet.

35 · A Surprise Guest

Zinnie was doing her best to avoid Marigold, which wasn't easy in a house as small as Aunt Sunny's. It would have been no problem in L.A., with their busy schedules and separate bedrooms, but in Pruet it was nearly impossible. If they were going to get through the rest of their time here without fighting, however, Zinnie thought it would be best if they just gave each other plenty of room.

And Marigold was out of her mind if she thought Zinnie was going to be able to write some kind of performance in the next few days! She had a blog! After she'd slept on it, she decided that there was no way she was going to give up on her dream of being editor in chief of *Muses*, even now that Madison's blog now had 1,350 shares (Zinnie had a hard time keeping herself from checking). She was just going to have to make this the best blog that she could. Maybe there was some way she could get her blog featured on Huzzah too, though that seemed very unlikely.

Luckily, she had the legitimate excuse of her blog to keep her busy whenever Marigold accosted her about writing something for her to direct for the tricentennial. As far as Zinnie was concerned, Marigold had gotten herself into that situation and she was going to have to get herself out! Zinnie had finally reworked the piece about the fun fourteenth by simply calling it "The Camping Trip" and not including Marigold in the narrative. It was all about the canoe. She had gone over it so many times, she knew it was in good shape, but she still thought it was the weakest of her posts so far. She guessed that was the price of leaving out the truth.

She'd also been wondering why Max hadn't just come out by now and told her he was Brave13. It couldn't be anyone else, could it? she wondered with a shudder. Maybe he was feeling shy about it because he liked her as much as she liked him. Once again the sweet, shivery love song feeling came over her. She was on her way to check her email, her laptop tucked under her arm, when Marigold tapped her on the shoulder.

"Yes?" Zinnie asked.

"We need to work on our performance today," Marigold said.

"I already told you," Zinnie said. "I can't help with that."

"Come on, you can just write a play, can't you?" Marigold asked. "You can just step away once you're done. I'm going to be the director."

"No," Zinnie said. "I can't write a play when I'm so focused on something else—like my blog."

"We still have four days," Marigold said. "I don't know why you're being so stubborn."

Lily poked her head around the corner. "You two need to be nice to each other."

"You can write something yourself," Zinnie said.

"Fine," Marigold said. "Maybe I will."

Zinnie went to the backyard and checked her email. There was a message from Brave13. Yes!

Next on your list, the water tower! But not the new water tower— the old one. Very important distinction. Oh, and the afternoon is the best time to go.

Brave13 once again attached a link to a map, and Zinnie had her next adventure. A message popped on her screen. It was Max! Her heart fluttered, and sure enough, she was back in the land of hearts and rainbows, vibrating like a hummingbird sipping pollen from a hot-pink hibiscus. The idea of Brave13 being a mystery had been fun for a while, but now she just wanted to let go of the game and talk about all the places he had sent her and why. She could only imagine what it would feel like to actually share her feelings. All she knew about being in love, or at least in like, revolved around her emotions being private. They were bubbling up now, like a soda can that had been shaken, and she thought she might explode if she didn't open up to Max. She beamed as she saw his words appear on the screen of her laptop.

Max: Hi!

Zinnie: Hi Max! The water tower's next, huh?

Max: Next for what?

Zinnie: My blog!

Max: What do you mean?

Zinnie: I don't want to ruin the mystery, but I think I should tell you that I know it's you. And it's the best, sweetest thing in the world!

Max: Uh . . .

Zinnie: Don't be shy! I'm so happy about it!

Max: Happy about what?

Zinnie: That you've been sending me all these secret emails about places in Pruet! I know you like me, and guess what? I like you, too!

Max: Zinnie, I really don't know what you're talking about. I read your blog because my grandpa told me about it, but I didn't send you those clues. Seriously.

Zinnie: So you didn't send me a bunch of messages about
liking me?
Max: No.

Zinnie felt the color drain from her face. Her stomach tightened and churned.

Zinnie: Really?
Max: It wasn't me.
Zinnie: I gotta go!

Zinnie signed off before Max could even reply. She was so embarrassed she felt like her whole body was changing color, from beet red to ghost white to a dull shade of green. She put her head between her knees, trying not to faint with humiliation. How could she have been so wrong about everything? And why had she revealed her feelings for him before she'd been absolutely certain that he felt the same way? Her ears started to ring. She bet this was some kind of rule of romance—"Don't announce your feelings about the other person until you have real proof that they like you, too." It was probably a rule that Marigold knew. Ugh, Marigold would have never made this mistake! As annoying as Marigold had been lately, and as unfair as she'd been about the fun fourteenth, Zinnie wished now that she'd asked her older sister for more advice about boyfriends and girlfriends. Maybe it would've stopped her from experiencing this moment of feeling like a snail, struggling to get its whole body inside its shell. She now understood what all those heartbreak songs were about on the radio.

After her panic had passed, but still with the weight of disappointment hanging on her like a wet beach towel, Zinnie closed her laptop and went to the kitchen, where Aunt Sunny had surely baked some snacks. Cookies could solve most anything. At least, up until now they had been able to. Sure enough, there was a plate of pecan sandies on the counter. She ate two. They did help a little, but not as much as Zinnie hoped.

Later, Zinnie rode on the red bike out to the old water tower. She saw it from a distance and had to leave her bike by the road and then walk a while up a little hill to reach it. She climbed the many stairs to the top, and just when she reached the top she heard a voice say, "You're here!"

She looked up and saw Chloe.

"Chloe! What are you doing here?" Zinnie asked.

"What do you mean? I'm the one who told you to come," Chloe said.

"Huh?" Zinnie asked.

"I'm Brave13," Chloe said with a smile.

"You are?" Zinnie asked. Chloe did a little bow. Zinnie put her hands over her mouth with surprise.

"Isn't this place the best?" Chloe asked, opening her

arms to gesture to the three-hundred-and-sixty-degree view all around them. Zinnie had to admit it was the best view in all of Pruet. She snapped some pictures for her blog.

"I thought it was the perfect place for a picnic," Chloe said, and held up a paper bag. She pulled out some quinoa salad, strawberries, and iced green tea. "I even brought us a picnic blanket." Chloe spread out a blanket for them.

"Want a strawberry?" Chloe asked. "I got them from Featherbrook Farm. Great post, by the way. I was laughing like crazy about the attack goose."

"Featherbrook Farm is awesome," Zinnie said, taking a strawberry. It was flavorful and sweet, and the juices dripped down her chin. "All the places you've sent me to have been. But I have to ask . . . why?"

"That first day I met you, you looked like you needed a muse," Chloe said, popping a strawberry into her mouth. "And then, I don't know, I just thought it was working so well. Your blog posts are so good that I thought I'd keep going."

"Why didn't you just tell me it was you?" Zinnie said, sipping some green tea. It was bitter; nothing like Aunt Sunny's sweet sun tea.

"Would you have thought I was a good muse if you knew who I was?" Chloe asked.

"Probably not," Zinnie agreed. After all, hadn't half

 224

the fun been imagining it was Max? "But wait. How do you know about all these places? You're not from here."

"My uncle and I have been doing location scouting for weeks," Chloe said. "You know, like before people shoot a movie, they go to the place where they're going to film it and look at all the possible locations for scenes. My uncle loves to take me because he says that kids can see things that adults don't."

"I wonder why that is," Zinnie said. The comment made her think of Lily, who did seem to be able to see what others couldn't.

"Nadia says we're more open human beings, less likely to be worried about something or thinking about the future. She says we live in the moment, so the world reveals itself to us." Chloe smiled.

"Wow," Zinnie said. "That's so cool. That's, like, one of the coolest things I've ever heard." It was conversations like this that made her want to be friends with Chloe in the first place. Zinnie had intuited that they had a connection, and she'd been right. "Do you mind if I include that in my blog?"

"Of course not!" Chloe said, and laughed. "That's what I like about you."

"What?" Zinnie said. The wind picked up, and a group of clouds puffed across the sky like horses.

"You're so not like the kids I know in L.A. They all

care so much about what other people think of them. They'd be like, 'Oh yeah, I already knew that.' They don't want to look uncool."

"What are you trying to say?" Zinnie asked, suspicious of where this was headed. She'd never thought of herself as "cool" but she didn't want other people to think that. Or if they did, she didn't want them to tell her!

"Just that I like you," Chloe said with an easy laugh.

Zinnie believed her. "I just did something really embarrassing," she said. The surprise of seeing Chloe had momentarily made her forget about what had just happened with Max.

"Tell me," Chloe said. Her teeth were red from the strawberries.

"I thought that someone else was Brave13—a boy," Zinnie said, burying her face in her hands.

"What's so embarrassing about that?" Chloe asked. "Did you ask him if he was?"

"Not only did I ask him, I basically announced that I liked him, you know, in *that* way, and told him that I knew he liked me, too." Already Zinnie was feeling a little better telling someone about this.

"What did he say?" Chloe asked.

"He said it wasn't him," Zinnie said. "Oh, if only I'd come to the water tower first and seen you, I would have saved myself from the single most embarrassing moment of my life!"

"Did he say how he felt about you?" Chloe asked.

"Not really—he just didn't respond to that part. That can only mean one thing, right? That he doesn't like me in *that* way?"

"Not necessarily," Chloe said. "I found out before I came here that this boy at my old school had had a crush on me since the second grade. I never even had a clue. And this boy had once seen me throw up my Halloween candy at recess. Talk about embarrassing!"

Chloe laughed and Zinnie did, too. It felt good— necessary, even—to share this experience with someone who understood.

"Do you like him as a boyfriend?" Zinnie asked.

"I'm not really into boyfriends and stuff like that," Chloe said.

"I didn't think I was either, until I met Max. Do you think there's a chance he still likes me?" Zinnie asked.

"For sure," Chloe said. "Maybe he didn't say anything because you kind of surprised him, is all. Maybe he likes you for the same reason I do—because you're not trying to be cool."

"So you don't think I'm cool?"

"OMG, that's not what I meant!" Chloe said, resting a hand on Zinnie's arm. "Exactly the opposite. I think you're so cool because you're not trying to be something you're not. You're not trying to impress anyone like . . . Well. Never mind." Chloe's face changed for a second.

"Like who?" Zinnie asked.

"Well, to be honest, like Marigold," Chloe said.

"She does think she's so cool," Zinnie said. She'd had it up to her eyeballs with her sister, and though she didn't realize it until this moment, keeping it to herself had been weighing on her. "She cares what everyone else thinks—a lot. Especially about her clothes."

"I feel like she wants to impress me because she wants to get to my uncle or something," Chloe said.

"She wants to impress you," Zinnie said, a little taken aback. "But it's more just because she wants to be friends with you."

"She's a lot to deal with sometimes," Chloe said. "No offense. She's what Nadia would call 'toxic.'"

"She is," Zinnie said, thinking of how unfair and mean Marigold had been lately. She knew she was treading on dangerous ground, but she was so fed up with Marigold that talking about her flaws was making Zinnie feel a little lighter. "Right now she's driving me crazy."

"In what way?" Chloe asked, handing her another strawberry.

"She's blaming things on me that aren't my fault—at all. She's bossing me around like I'm her personal assistant. And she doesn't seem to care about my work at all."

"I really hope she doesn't follow me around PAM next year," Chloe said. "The only reason I'm hanging out with her now is because it's the summer."

"She probably won't follow you at PAM," Zinnie said. What had felt like sweet relief was taking on a sour tinge. "She's not actually mean, you know. Just to me, but I'm her sister, and sisters do that sometimes."

"I wouldn't know," Chloe said. "I'm an only child."

"Sisters can be pretty rough with one another. I do it too—though she is way worse. And she's not fake or anything. She does want to be friends with you."

"I don't think she's, like, a bad person," Chloe said. "It's just that I'd really rather hang out with you, and she's kind of a pain. You understand, right?"

Zinnie nodded, but couldn't look her in the eye.

"You know what? I really should go," Zinnie said. The guilt of having said mean things about her sister was starting to build. "I need to get back to my aunt's."

"Oh, okay," Chloe said. "I was kind of hoping we could go to the beach—without Marigold, of course."

A memory came to Zinnie: Marigold, crying in Mom's arms because the Cuties had been mean to her. There was nothing worse than seeing her older sister cry.

"No, I need to get back to my family now, but thanks for all the amazing tips," Zinnie said with a smile that made her cheeks ache.

"Uh, okay," Chloe said. "Bye, I guess."

"Bye," Zinnie said as she scurried down the water tower's ladder, eager to get on her bike and ride.

36 · Working Together

Marigold was helping get things ready for dinner while also trying to brainstorm possibilities for the tricentennial performance when Zinnie, brow creased, came into the backyard. She had been out on one of her writing adventures—getting more writing material. This was Zinnie's mission in life, yet she couldn't help Marigold come up with any ideas. Marigold had just this morning quickly read over Zinnie's posts on her iPad, just to make sure that Zinnie wasn't writing about her. And she wasn't, thank goodness. Zinnie had been true to her word. The only sister she'd written about was Lily in a funny post about the bison.

"You know what?" Zinnie said.

"What?" Marigold asked as she set out the picnic blanket in the backyard. They were getting ready for an outdoor dinner. Tony was going to grill some hamburgers, and Peter, Mack, and Jean were coming over. Marigold was hoping that Peter, having had more time to cool off and think about what she'd said, might be a little more open about how he was feeling. She was also hoping that he wouldn't ask for too many details about whatever the Silver sisters were planning on doing for the tricentennial, because she had no clue, even though she was determined to cement in his mind that they weren't just summer people.

As if Zinnie could hear her thoughts, she approached Marigold and helped her straighten the edge of the picnic blanket. "I'll help you figure out something for the tricentennial."

"You will?" Marigold asked, surprised.

"Yes," Zinnie said. "And I'm sorry."

"You are?" Marigold asked.

"I'm sorry that I told Peter about Chloe. I honestly didn't know," Zinnie said.

"It's okay," Marigold said, though she was slightly suspicious. Zinnie's current attitude was such a change from this morning. But having just been on the opposite side of the apology with Peter, Marigold knew how important it was to respond. "I forgive you. And I'm sorry, too. I shouldn't have reacted the way I did."

"It's okay," Zinnie said, and wrapped her arms around her sister in a bear hug.

"Um, is something else going on?" Marigold asked.

"Yeah," Zinnie said. She bit her lip, staring at the

ground, and then spoke. "Max and I were messaging, and I thought he was Brave13 and that it meant that he liked me, but I was wrong. It wasn't him." She hid her face in her hands. "I basically told him I liked him, and he didn't say he felt the same."

"Wait, he's *not* Brave13?" Marigold asked.

"No," Zinnie said, peeking from between her fingers.

"Then who is?" Marigold asked. Zinnie shrugged, still covering her face.

"Who else could it be?" Marigold said.

"Dunno." Zinnie busied herself with the picnic blanket. "But I'm pretty embarrassed."

"I don't know much about boyfriends," Marigold said, sensing her sister's distress. "But I don't think they think about these things the way we do."

"Do you have any advice?" Zinnie asked.

Marigold put a hand on her hip and thought. "Pretend it didn't happen."

"Really?" Zinnie asked. "But it did happen."

"It happened for you, but did it happen for him?" Marigold said, feeling wise and older sisterly.

"I have no idea what you even mean by that," Zinnie said.

"I mean if you act like everything is normal, then maybe it will just . . . be normal again," Marigold said. Zinnie didn't look convinced.

"Is everything okay over here?" Lily asked, stepping

outside with plates, napkins, and utensils.

"Yeah," Marigold said. "We're cool."

"We're just talking about what we should do about the tricentennial performance," Zinnie said.

"It should be fun and upbeat," Marigold said. "It's a celebration."

"We need to write a song," Lily said.

"That would be good," Marigold said. "Except we can't sing. Important detail."

"Maybe a rap?" Zinnie said.

Marigold shrugged. "Eh, I don't know about that."

"A poem? Like, spoken word?" Zinnie suggested.

"Oh, I know!" Marigold said. "We can interview people about what they love about Pruet and put it together somehow."

"Good idea," Zinnie said. "Wait a second, did you get that idea from Madison's blog?"

"So what if I did?" Marigold said. "This is totally different."

"I guess you're right," Zinnie said. "It's not like Madison invented interviewing."

"Maybe we can act it out," Lily said.

"And Chloe can do the choreography," Marigold said.

"No," Zinnie said firmly.

"Whoa," Marigold said, sensing some hostility.

"It's just that you're the director, right?" Zinnie

asked. "You want to be crowned Eliza Pruet, don't you?"

"How'd you know?" Marigold asked.

"Give me a break," Zinnie said. "I'm your sister."

Later, as they ate their picnic of hamburgers, cucumber salad, and sliced tomatoes from the garden, Marigold interviewed everyone about what they loved most about Pruet.

"All the animals who live here," Lily said. "Oh, and the people, too."

"I love the sailing," Peter added. His mood was definitely better than it had been last night. The best part was that because she had told him the whole truth from her end, she was at ease. "But I guess everybody already knows that."

"A history of various buildings around Pruet would also be interesting," Tony said.

"It sounds like everyone has their own opinions," Aunt Sunny said.

"And they're all pretty different," Jean added.

"Maybe that's it, though," Marigold said. "Maybe if we combine all our favorite things about Pruet, you can put that together to write the song, Zinnie."

"Don't even think about asking me to play the guitar, okay?" Peter said. And everyone laughed, remembering his reluctant performance in the talent show the girls had put on their first summer here.

"Some people just don't like performing," Aunt Sunny said. "I know it might be hard for you girls, especially those of you headed to the Performing Arts Magnet, to understand, but it is true."

"Luckily, I do," Tony said. "The only thing I don't do very well is compose original tunes. That's why Tony and the Contractors is a cover band."

"I bet Max could do it," Marigold said. Of course! That was the perfect solution. He could sing, the sisters could act it out, and Marigold would direct. She glanced at Zinnie, who was shaking her head "no." But Marigold just smiled at her reassuringly. Naturally Zinnie would have to be the one to ask him. She'd work on that later.

"Marigold, do you want to go for a walk with me?" Peter asked.

"Sure," Marigold said. "Let's go to the pear orchard."

With a clear view of the night sky, it was the perfect spot to set things straight again.

"I've been thinking about what you said," he said as they walked through the evening air, which had cooled as the sun had lowered, was full of the scent of Aunt Sunny's flowers, and now hummed with insects.

"What part of what I said?" Marigold asked. "I kind of said a lot."

"All of it, I guess," Peter said as they passed beneath the stone archway. "There was this guy in my class in fifth grade, Jeremy. Man, what a jerk. He decided that because I had red hair he was going to call me Big Red, which everyone thought was pretty funny because I was the second shortest person in the class."

"That's so mean," Marigold said. "Is he still in your class?"

"He is, but he doesn't bother me anymore. Not since I joined the sailing team. The worst part was, he had been one of my best friends in fourth grade. In fifth grade I had a hard time with friends, and it was not a good year," Peter said.

"So you understand—maybe—a little?" Marigold asked, taking a seat on the stone bench.

"Yeah," Peter said, sitting next to her. The bench wasn't very big. And yet, Marigold thought, he didn't necessarily have to sit so very close to her. "I think so. You knew I might not be like, 'Nice to meet you, niece of Mr. Rathbone. Welcome to Pruet.'"

"Exactly," Marigold said. They chuckled. Peter held her gaze, and she felt her insides melt.

"So I'm sorry I was kind of stubborn when we were out by the ri-vah," he said. Marigold swooned at his accent.

"And I was also thinking about how you said you wanted to spend more time with me," Peter said. Marigold felt her color rise. "And that was sweet. Wicked sweet." Marigold's pulse quickened. "'Cause I want to spend more time with you, too."

He leaned toward her, and she closed her eyes, anticipating the kiss she had imagined for so long. But just then she heard Lily's voice.

"Marigold! Marigold!" Lily called. "Aunt Sunny made us brownies and Tony has his guitar and everyone is singing Beatles songs. You have to come back!"

"We'll be right there, Lily," Marigold said, hoping Lily might leave. But she stayed there waiting until Marigold and Peter gave her their full attention. "Okay, we're coming." Marigold and Peter smiled at each other as they stood up and headed back toward everyone else. At least they had five more nights.

Marigold interviewed the Pasques more about their favorite things about Pruet before they went home for the evening. Then she asked Aunt Sunny, Tony, and her sisters to go into great detail about what made this little town so special to them. After she had several notebook pages filled with ideas, and when the sisters were getting ready for bed, Marigold begged Zinnie to ask Max about singing the song.

"He has such a great voice, and you two do write really creative things together."

"I feel so weird about Max right now!" Zinnie said. "You do it!"

"But you guys are friends, and the thing you like to do most together is make up songs. Look—I got all the information for you," she said, handing over a few pieces of paper with everyone's favorite things about Pruet written on it. "These words are perfect, but it's no fun unless it's set to music. You and Max can do that better than anyone."

"But what about the fact that I just told him I liked him? Oh, I'm so embarrassed just thinking about it!" Zinnie said, hiding her face in her pillow.

"Here's what I've learned about being embarrassed," Marigold said, sitting on the edge of her sister's bed. She had plenty of experience with the subject. In seventh grade she'd bragged to all her friends about being in a blockbuster movie and then felt like an idiot when her scene was cut. "The more embarrassed you act, the more awkward it gets. If you just move on, everyone else will, too."

"So, like you were saying before, pretend like it never happened?" Zinnie asked.

"Pretty much," Marigold said.

"I don't know, Marigold. It definitely did happen— I really think it'd be better if you did this," Zinnie said. "This is your project, after all."

"But you're so good at stuff like this—and Max has such a good voice and is so charming. And you and Max together? You're like chocolate and peanut butter. A perfect combination."

Zinnie shook her head.

"Please," Marigold said. "I'm your sister, and I'm asking you from the bottom of my heart."

Zinnie thought for a moment and then said, "Okay. As your sister."

"Thank you," Marigold said, wrapping her arms around Zinnie. "As family we have to have each other's backs, right?"

"Right," Zinnie said, though she looked like she was going to cry.

"Wait. Do you want me to talk to him first?" Marigold asked.

"No," Zinnie said. "I can handle this. I can do it for my sister."

"Are you sure?" Marigold asked.

"Sure," Zinnie said. "I'll do it right now." And she and Marigold took her laptop into the backyard and typed a message to Max.

37 · The New Plan

Marigold had walked with Zinnie over to the yacht club a little early so they could watch the TV crew transform it back to its usual state. They sat on a picnic bench as the workers loaded up the trucks with lights and equipment. Inside, the crew carried the usual chairs and tables back into the dining room while others replaced the drapes and rehung pictures. They were due to return the yacht club back to the people of Pruet by the end of the morning.

This was not going to be an easy video chat with Max.

As Zinnie sat in Jean's office, laptop at the ready, Zinnie felt as tense as the ball of elastic bands that Aunt Sunny kept in her kitchen drawer.

But what else could she do when her sister asked her something from the bottom of her heart? If Marigold knew that she'd been talking about her behind her back with Chloe, she'd be devastated.

So last night, with Marigold coaching her to "just act normal," she'd messaged Max, seeing if he'd help her write a song for the tricentennial. She didn't even mention their last message exchange. Zinnie heard back from him first thing in the morning. He'd replied, "Sure!" He'd also mentioned that they'd probably need to video chat, as it would be a lot easier to write a song together if they could actually see each other.

"Does noon Pruet time work for you?" Zinnie had asked.

"Yup!" Max had written. "See you then!"

"I bet you can use Jean's office at the yacht club. The Wi-Fi is pretty good there," Marigold had said. "She goes home for lunch at noon, so maybe you can suggest that as a time."

She'd been feeling better about the situation. He wasn't acting any differently. Maybe Marigold was right. She could just pretend it didn't happen and all of her embarrassment would go away.

As she waited for a few minutes for noon to arrive, though, she realized that even if she could make the embarrassment go away, her feelings were still hurt. He didn't like her in the same way, and that just didn't feel good. It had been better to have the question hanging in the air. As her computer screen brightened to life with the incoming request to video chat, she was instantly aware that she wasn't over her embarrassment after all.

"I'll wait for you outside, okay?" Marigold asked.

Zinnie nodded. She felt herself blush and her hands grow clammy, and she couldn't stop bouncing her knees. She took a deep breath and answered the call. Max's megawatt smile lit up her screen.

"Hi! Where are you?" Max asked. He seemed pretty normal.

"I'm, um, at the yacht club," Zinnie said. She picked up her computer to give him a view of the harbor.

"That's awesome!" he said. "Check this out." She watched on his screen as he showed her canals with narrow boats on them.

"Wow! Where are you exactly?" Zinnie asked. So far, so good. If they could just talk about everything else but the embarrassing conversation, maybe this would be okay.

"Venice, Italy," Max said. "My dad is stationed in Vincenza, and Mom and I decided to spend a few nights here before my dad joins us and we fly to Boston. Isn't this place cool?"

"It's amazing," Zinnie said as a breeze came through the window. The air felt cool and fresh. The wind carried the salty smell of the sea and whiffs of something floral her way—honeysuckle, she thought.

 243

"So we're going to write a song," Max said.

"Yeah," Zinnie said, and held up her notebook. "I have all these ideas here. We just need to turn them into something good."

"Okay, let me grab my guitar," Max said, leaving Zinnie with the view from the balcony of his hotel room. She drew several deep breaths while she had the chance. A few moments later, Max reappeared on the screen with his guitar. As he bowed his head to tune it, Zinnie noticed that his hair was longer. He was so cute! Especially when he was concentrating on something. He began to strum a happy tune.

"How's this?" he asked.

Zinnie nodded her head along with the beat. "Something a little slower, maybe?"

He slowed it down a little, and with his pinkie, plucked a few high notes. "That's perfect," Zinnie said.

Max kept playing and said, "Let's hear some words." Zinnie felt a little rush of excitement as she recognized the playful glimmer in Max's eyes. "I'll start. There's a list of reasons to love Pruet . . . ," he sang.

"We don't possibly have time to go through it," Zinnie sang in response. She was tone deaf, but she did the best she could. Max laughed a little as he strummed again.

"But we can start at the top and see how it goes," Max said.

"And where we'll end up, nobody knows," Zinnie said. Max wrinkled his nose. "Not quite right—let's try again. What rhymes with 'goes' . . . ? 'Nose'? 'Bows'? 'Shows'?"

"I'll play again and just see what comes to your mind," Max said.

"Feel the Pruet love from your head to your toes," Zinnie sang.

"Yes!" Max said.

Zinnie and Max sang for another hour, working though the list of everything she and her sisters had come up with until they had a rough draft.

"I'll finish it tonight and email it ASAP," Zinnie said. "Will you be able to practice with us, like, as soon as you get here?"

"You bet. I'll see you soon!"

"I can't wait," Zinnie said before she could stop herself. Her cheeks turned pink.

"Me either," Max said. "Listen, about the other day, when you told me—"

"Never mind," Zinnie said. "Just forget all about it, okay? I didn't mean it."

"Really?" Max asked.

Zinnie nodded.

"I'd better go," Max said. "That was fun."

"It was," said Zinnie. They signed off. Zinnie closed her computer and then slumped on top of it. How was she going to continue to hide her feelings when he was so adorable?

When she walked out of the yacht club, Marigold was waiting for her on the lawn, watching the crew pack up the last of the set.

"How'd it go?" Marigold asked.

"Good," Zinnie said.

"See, I told you it would be okay!" Marigold said as the last of Mr. Rathbone's crew trucks rolled out of the parking lot.

38 · A Morning Full of Good Ideas

T he next morning Marigold couldn't wait for Zinnie to wake up so she could show her what she'd been working on all night. The night before, Zinnie had made Marigold promise that she would let her sleep in the next day.

"I promise I'll have something good for you," Zinnie had told her. "But I don't know how long it will take me tonight."

"Okay," Marigold had said. "I'll wait for you to wake up on your own."

But now she was pacing. It was almost nine thirty, and they still had to photocopy the maps for the Historical Society's tour and fold the brochures for the Piping Plover Society's exhibits.

"Here you go," Zinnie said when she came down the stairs. She handed her song lyrics to Marigold.

"There are four verses and a chorus," Zinnie explained as Marigold read them over. "Max will sing the verses and play the guitar."

"Zinnie, this is perfect," Marigold said as she shoveled a spoonful of cereal into her mouth. She couldn't believe how sweet and funny, not to mention *actable*, the lyrics were. "Thank you so much. It's like all the verses are little scenes about what's great about Pruet."

"That was the plan," Zinnie said as she poured herself a bowl of Cheerios and added a heaping teaspoon of sugar. "That way we can act them out while Max sings. Where's Aunt Sunny?"

"She and Tony are out on a morning walk," Marigold said as she read over the lyrics once again. "This is going to work so well. And guess what? I have good news, too."

"What's that?" Zinnie asked as Lily entered the kitchen, all dressed and ready for camp.

"I texted Chloe last night, and she said she would be happy to help with choreography," Marigold said. "With all of her experience with Mr. Rathbone, I think she'll help us look really polished and professional."

"I love that idea!" Lily said.

"We don't need Chloe for that," Zinnie said. "We can do it ourselves."

"What do you have against Chloe all of a sudden?" Marigold asked. Zinnie had always seemed to be dying to hang out with Chloe.

"Nothing," Zinnie said, though Marigold could tell she was hiding something. Was Zinnie just jealous? "I just don't think we need her for that, is all. You'll be a great director. Besides, you want to be Eliza Pruet, remember? You need to make sure that you're the one who gets the credit for this."

"Hmmm. Maybe you're right," Marigold said. "Though I still want to hang out with her today." Marigold pulled out her phone and started texting, but Zinnie grabbed her phone away from her.

"No," Zinnie said. "Don't."

"Hey," Marigold said, taking her phone back. "What's your problem? Just because you're not going to school with Chloe and can't be best friends with her doesn't mean you have to ruin my—" But just then they heard Aunt Sunny and Tony coming through the front door. They had made it this long without fighting in front of Aunt Sunny. Marigold wasn't going to break her promise now.

"I don't have a problem," Zinnie whispered. "I just think we can do a great job on our own."

"The important thing is that we all have fun," Lily said through gritted teeth.

"Exactly, Lily. I appreciate your input, Zinnie, but I'm allowed to hang out with who I want to."

Aunt Sunny and Tony, all rosy cheeks and smiles, walked into the kitchen just as Marigold hit "send."

"Good morning, girls," Aunt Sunny said as she

poured herself a cup of decaf and started making her special coffee.

"Good morning," the girls answered in an overly cheerful unison.

"How was your walk?" Marigold asked.

"Glorious—I'm so relieved that Mr. Rathbone and his people have left so that we can have some peace again. Nothing against him personally," Tony said, "but it's nice to have our sleepy town back."

"The walk by the harbor was especially invigorating. Tony and I have just had a marvelous idea," Aunt Sunny said.

"That's so funny," Marigold said. "We've all had good ideas this morning."

"Must be something in the air," Tony said, and offered Aunt Sunny some sugar for her coffee before pouring his own.

"The festivities for the tricentennial kick off on Friday afternoon. And as you know, your parents and Max and his folks are arriving that morning," Aunt Sunny began. "But the big clambake isn't until after the regatta on Saturday. There's nothing planned for Friday night."

"So, we thought we'd throw a little party at the lighthouse," Tony said. "For our family and dearest friends—the Pasques."

"Yay!" the girls all cheered.

"We'll have fresh lobsters," Tony said. "It'll be a blast."

"I love lobster," Zinnie said.

"Can I invite Chloe?" Marigold asked.

"Aunt Sunny said the party was for our dearest friends only," Zinnie said.

"Do you consider Chloe a dear friend?" Aunt Sunny asked.

"I do," Marigold said.

"Then by all means, ask her to come," Aunt Sunny said.

Marigold gave a worried-looking Zinnie a triumphant look and sent her friend another text.

39 · Can't Fool a Sister

"I read your blog post about the water tower," Chloe said to Zinnie privately when she came over to Aunt Sunny's at Marigold's invitation. "How come you didn't mention I was Brave13?"

Zinnie was surprising even herself with her productivity. She'd been able to squeeze in another blog post right after breakfast but before she and Marigold had dropped off Lily. She felt differently about all of her adventures now that she knew it was Chloe who had given her the tips. She'd debated even writing about the water tower. After all, this adventure contained the climax of her whole blog—the revealed identity of the mysterious Brave13. She didn't want to deny that to her readers. At the same time it would really hurt Marigold's feelings if she knew the truth.

She was not about to do that to her sister—again.

She'd come up with a compromise. She would write about her visit to the water tower (the panoramic pictures were too good not to post), but leave out the part about Chloe. Instead, she would focus on the journey of getting there, the rickety steps to the top, and the moment she thought she might fall off.

"I think that might hurt my sister's feelings," Zinnie whispered, looking over her shoulder at her sister, who was preparing a tray of lemonade and cookies.

"I get that you're sisters, but you and I are allowed to have our own friendship, right? It's not like she's the boss of you—even if she thinks she is."

"I know," Zinnie said.

"I'm not sure what your favorite kind of cookie is," Marigold called from the kitchen. "So I'm arranging an assortment—all homemade, of course."

"Thanks," Chloe said, and then leaned in a little closer to Zinnie. "Is she going to be following us everywhere at the lighthouse party?"

Now Zinnie really felt sick. If Marigold could hear this conversation, she wouldn't just be angry, she'd be heartbroken. She really liked Chloe—she was adventurous and original and creative and smart—but going behind her sister's back was making Zinnie uneasy in her own skin.

"You know what?" Zinnie said. "I don't think you

should come to that party anymore."

"Why?" Chloe asked, confused. "I thought we were friends."

"We are," Zinnie whispered.

"But I feel like you want me to leave," Chloe responded in a full voice.

"I'm sorry," Zinnie whispered again. "I just don't think it's a good idea for you to come to the party."

"Uh, Zinnie?" Marigold called from the kitchen. "I could use some help over here! Can you move this table? And Chloe, please don't leave, just sit down and make yourself comfortable."

"It's better if we don't talk about this anymore," Zinnie said to Chloe.

"Don't you think you're being a little rude to Chloe?" Marigold asked Zinnie in a harsh whisper as she pulled her sister aside.

"No," Zinnie said.

"Then why did she say it seemed like you wanted her to leave?" Marigold said. "She's never going to want to come over to our house this fall if she thinks we're rude."

"Okay, I'm confused," Zinnie said, trying to avoid the real conflict. "First, you didn't want me to hang out with her at all, and now you want me to be her friend all of a sudden?"

"Oh, come on," Marigold said. "Just because I wanted some time alone with her doesn't mean I want you to be mean. There's a huge difference and you know it."

"Sorry," Zinnie said. Marigold was right. She did know the difference. But the situation was so much more complicated than Marigold knew. There was no way she was going to tell Marigold the truth. It would crush her, especially after the year with the Cuties. "I guess I'm just a little stressed out because Madison's blog has way more hits than mine, and I don't think my last entries were very good. It's been going downhill ever since the bison."

"Are you sure that's it?" Marigold said.

"I'm positive," Zinnie said, avoiding her sister's gaze. "You know how much I want to be editor in chief of *Muses*."

"Everything okay?" Chloe asked from the living room.

"Just fine," Marigold said, and they peeked around the corner.

Chloe looked wounded. Zinnie's stomach knotted up. It was clear all of a sudden—Chloe didn't have a sister so she didn't understand the position that Zinnie was in or how Zinnie could both not be able to stand Marigold and love her fiercely at the very same time. All Chloe understood was that she'd been uninvited to the lighthouse party.

 255

"Just one second! We'll be right in!" Then Marigold turned to Zinnie. "I feel like you're hiding something."

"Nope," Zinnie said, trying her best to look relaxed.

"You think you can fool me, but you can't. I'm your sister," Marigold said with a satisfied smile. "I know what it is."

"You do?" Zinnie asked, her stomach dropping.

"Yep," Marigold said, nodding her head. "It's Max! Of course! He's coming tomorrow, and you're freaking out."

"Things went fine on our video chat," Zinnie said. "I followed your advice and just acted normal, and it was okay."

"I get it, Zin," Marigold said, and gave Zinnie a squeeze. "You're afraid that even though you got through that video chat okay, you're going to act super-weird when you see him in person. Plus, with him not liking you back, you're worried you won't even be friends anymore. I totally understand."

"That's not it," Zinnie said, though it hadn't occurred to her that she'd be so nervous and weird that she and Max wouldn't even be able to have a friendship. The best thing about hanging out with him was that she always found herself being even more creative and funny than she already was.

"Let's get out of this pantry," Marigold said. "And now that we've figured out the root of your odd behavior, do you think you could at least try to be nice to Chloe, while, you know, still giving us some space?"

"Sure," Zinnie said, feeling more anxious than ever. "I mean, I'll try."

40 · The Power of Suggestion

I'm not nervous, Zinnie told herself the next day as she heard a car rumbling down the driveway and a few moments later Max's voice calling out, "We're here!"

She was up in the attic bathroom, brushing her hair, trying to push out the anxious thoughts that Marigold had put into her head. The power of suggestion was what her dad called it when she didn't crave something until she saw a commercial for it. This was weirdly similar. Until Marigold had put the idea in her mind, Zinnie hadn't considered that her feelings for Max would ruin her friendship with him. It was so unfair! She couldn't control that the thought of his smile made her heart race!

"Zinnie, Max is here!" Lily called from downstairs.

"I'm coming!" Zinnie replied, and gave herself a

firm look in the mirror. *Stop worrying,* she told herself silently as the butterflies in her stomach seemed to multiply. *This is* Max. *Your friend.*

"Zinnie!" Marigold called. "Max brought us something!"

"Okay," Zinnie said. She took a deep breath and smiled at her reflection. Hmm. She looked a little pale. She pinched her cheeks the way she'd seen Marigold do right before an audition and splashed some cold water on her face. Then she patted her skin dry and went downstairs.

At the very same moment that she rounded the corner of the stairwell, Max was running toward the kitchen, a box under his arm. Was this the surprise he'd been talking about? It had to be. Zinnie couldn't stop her body in time and they collided—hard.

"Whoops, sorry!" Zinnie said, wincing as she rubbed her head.

"No, I'm sorry. It was my fault," Max said, covering his eye with his hand. "I shouldn't have been running in the house. I was just excited to give this to you." He tapped the box. "Are you okay?"

"Yeah, I'm fine," Zinnie said, looking up and registering how close they were standing to each other. Max's face was just inches from her own. And he was . . . beautiful. His eyes had flecks of gold. They looked like the Pacific Ocean on a simmering summer afternoon—even though one of them was a little red and looked like it might be swelling. His light brown hair, which was longish now, had a blond streak in it from the sun. And his smile—she swore—was even bigger than last year!

"Was your flight hunky-dory?" Zinnie asked. Her stomach dropped. *Hunky-dory?* What kind of expression was that? She'd never said it before in her life! And what did it even mean?

"Uh . . . " Max looked confused.

"I mean, are you . . . I mean, did you . . . ?" Zinnie said, as tongue-tied as she'd ever been. "You made it here alive! And that's great!"

Oh no, she thought. *I am definitely acting weird.*

"Yeah," Max said. "That's definitely good. And here, I brought you this." He handed her the small, neatly wrapped box.

"Wow," Zinnie said, taking the box and opening it. Inside were a few sheets of royal-blue tissue paper and under those was the most beautiful notebook she'd ever seen in her life. It was small, about the size of a postcard. The paper inside was lined with gold. No one had ever given her a more perfect gift in her whole life. "This is so beautiful! Thank you so much. I absolutely love it!" As she held the gift in her hand, she believed for a shining moment that he liked her, too. And not just as a friend. Her breathing grew shallow. The world stopped spinning and righted itself.

"There you are, Zinnie," said Lily, who had come to

find her. "Don't you just love the notebooks that Max brought us?"

"'Us'?" Zinnie asked. The bump on her head throbbed.

"Yeah," said Marigold, who was right behind Lily. "They're so *Italian*. Lily's going to use hers for science observations, and I'm going to make directing notes in mine. What are you going to do with yours?"

"What I usually do," Zinnie said, her chin trembling. "I'm the one who always carries a notebook, remember?"

"Are you okay?" Max asked. He touched her arm.

"Yeah," Zinnie said, holding her breath so that she wouldn't cry. This wasn't the special, perfect just-for-her gift that she thought it was, and believing for those few golden seconds that it had been made the reality that much worse.

41 · Why Would She Say That?

Marigold hadn't realized how much she missed her parents until she saw them parking the mini-van. She'd been sitting by the window in the living room, waiting for them to arrive. And now joy washed over her like a gentle ocean wave as she ran to them. She really wanted them to meet Chloe, and maybe they could get Chloe's parents' information so that they could arrange a carpool. Also, she just wanted to hug them.

Lily and Zinnie followed her outside to greet them. As Mom and Dad stepped out of their rental car, the sisters covered them with hugs and kisses. Lily jumped right into her dad's arms. Zinnie wrapped her arms around her mom's waist, and Marigold pulled the whole family together into a bear hug.

"We've really missed you girls," Mom said, planting a big kiss on each of them.

"The house is way too quiet without you," Dad said as he unloaded suitcases from the back. "Have you been having fun?"

"Of course," Lily said. "We're in Pruet."

"I've been helping out with the tricentennial," Marigold said. "I was Jean's assistant. I did everything from setting up the ice cream social to getting a special permit for cooking on the beach from the town council to hanging paper lanterns—not to mention directing an act about why we love Pruet so much."

"Which Zinnie wrote with Max," Lily said.

"You wrote a play in addition to your blog?" Dad asked Zinnie.

"Just a song," Zinnie said.

"That's fun. I can't wait to see it," Mom said, pulling Marigold close. "I'm proud of you for directing. That's new."

"And I love the Young Naturalists," Lily said. "I wish it was my school!"

"That's so great, honey," Mom said, running her hands through Lily's curls.

"And Zinnie," Dad said, "I've been reading your blog. How's it going?"

"Just okay," Zinnie said.

Zinnie had been acting strange ever since Max

arrived. Marigold had been so right about how freaked out Zinnie was over her crush. It was really messing with her head! Their first rehearsal with Max had been pretty rough. Max played his guitar and sang while Zinnie, Lily, and Marigold joined in on the chorus, stepping forward in pairs to improvise the activities described in the lyrics.

But Zinnie was totally out of it, tripping not once but twice, forgetting the words to the chorus she'd written herself, and generally acting like she was present only in body. Her mind seemed to be in another place.

When Marigold had asked her if she was okay, she'd just said that she didn't want to talk about it. She'd stayed back at Aunt Sunny's while the rest of the family had taken a walk on the beach. This was especially weird, because Max was going, and Zinnie had been talking about seeing Max again ever since last summer.

"Just okay?" Dad said. Zinnie nodded. "The concept is great—I can't believe all the places you've discovered—and your pieces definitely have a strong voice. Have you found out who Brave13 is yet?"

"No," Zinnie said, staring at the ground. "That's part of the mystery."

"I think your audience is going to want to know," Dad said. "I know I do. You have to find out before you leave."

"I guess so," Zinnie said. "But maybe it's no big deal if I don't."

"No big deal?" Marigold asked. "I can't believe you just said that."

"I haven't gotten any emails recently. . . ." Zinnie said, her voice trailing off. "Besides, I don't even think I'm in the running for editor in chief. Madison's blog is the big hit of the summer. It was picked up by Huzzah."

"That's great for Madison," Dad said. "But that is not the only thing Mrs. Lee will be considering, I'm sure." He gave her an extra hug.

"Hello!" Aunt Sunny called from the doorway. Mom and Dad waved. "Come on in. Lunch is on the table."

"Great!" Dad called. "We haven't eaten anything all day except for those terrible airplane snack packs."

"We made tea sandwiches," Lily said, skipping ahead. "Cucumber and cream cheese, salmon and watercress, and tuna salad. We used cookie cutters to make them into shapes."

"Sounds perfect!" Mom said.

After lunch they all walked together to Edith's. As Mom and Dad marveled over Edith's new flavors, and Lily and Zinnie sampled some of the ones they hadn't tried yet, Marigold spotted Chloe walking by.

"Oh, Mom," Marigold said, pointing out the window. "Look. That's the girl I was telling you about. The one who's going to PAM next year!"

"I'd love to meet her," Mom said.

"I'll go get her," Marigold said. "You're going to see how cool she is."

"Can't wait!" Mom said.

Marigold darted down the street. Not only did she want to introduce Chloe to her parents, she also wanted to ask her for some directing tips, even though Zinnie didn't want Chloe's help. If Marigold wanted to be crowned Eliza Pruet, they needed all the help they could get. The song itself was charming, but somehow it wasn't coming together the way it needed to. She wouldn't even be considered for Eliza Pruet if the whole thing was a flop. Everyone would be there at the lighthouse party tonight, so they could have another rehearsal then, with Chloe there to offer her expert advice.

"Chloe!" Marigold called. Chloe turned around and gave her a sort of half smile, but she didn't stop walking. Marigold jogged to catch up to her. "I just wanted to say that I'm so happy you're coming to the party tonight," she said, slightly out of breath. "I really want to get your opinion on some of the last-minute choreography that I'm trying to put into place. The song that Zinnie and her friend Max came up with is so cute, but I want this to look as polished as possible. I know the performance is tomorrow, but I'm pretty sure that with just a few simple changes from your professional point of view, we can make it so much better."

"Oh . . . I'm not coming tonight," Chloe said.

"Really?" Marigold asked. "But I've told my parents all about you. I really want them to meet you. They said we might be able to carpool next year. . . . And we really do need your help for the choreography."

"I'm sorry. Didn't Zinnie tell you?" Chloe said.

"Tell me what?" Marigold asked.

"She told me that she didn't think it was a good idea for me to come tonight," Chloe said.

"She did what?" Marigold asked. Her sadness was quickly being replaced by anger. "Why would she say that?"

"Um, it's hard to explain," Chloe said. "Anyway, I'm meeting my uncle right now. A friend of his is sailing us over to the Vineyard tonight. So, I should probably get going. Sorry. See ya."

Marigold's heart pounded in her chest as she watched Chloe walk away.

42 · How Could You?

"Zinnie, I need to talk to you, okay?" Marigold said to her as soon as she walked through the door of the lighthouse. Aunt Sunny was right next to her, so Marigold had a big smile plastered on her face as she said it, but Zinnie could feel the anger under the surface. The live lobsters were climbing and squirming in the zipped-up canvas bags that Tony was holding. From Marigold's withering glance, Zinnie felt just like those lobsters probably did: trapped and angry and about to get boiled.

"Okay," Zinnie said, and checked out her surroundings. Mom and Dad were chopping vegetables for a salad in the tiny lighthouse kitchen, and Lily and Peter were playing jacks out on the porch. Max was doing cannonballs off the diving board, and his parents were sitting on the porch swing shucking corn. The girls had made it this far without a fight, so Zinnie doubted that Marigold was going to break now, especially not with so many witnesses.

"Let's go upstairs to the little room," Marigold said.

"But it's such a lovely evening," Aunt Sunny said. "How can you spend a minute indoors?"

"I know, Aunt Sunny," Marigold said. "It's just that the view from way up there is really inspiring. I think it will help us come up with the finishing touches for our performance tomorrow."

Aunt Sunny gave them a skeptical glance and then continued into the kitchen. Marigold took Zinnie's hand and practically dragged her up the narrow stairway.

"Ouch," Zinnie said when they got to the top of the stairs.

"How could you?" Marigold whispered angrily.

"How could I what?" Zinnie asked.

"Tell Chloe not to come tonight! You know I wanted to introduce her to Mom and Dad. You know how much I want to be friends with her."

"I didn't want—"

"I know, I know, for 'some reason'"—Marigold made air quotes with her fingers as she said this—"you just didn't want her to help at all. But I think I know what that reason is."

"I don't think you d—" Zinnie started.

"You're jealous!" Marigold said. "You've been jealous ever since I got cast on the TV show because you wanted to write about it in your blog. But instead of getting over it and being happy for me, you've tried to ruin everything."

"That's not fair," Zinnie said. "I haven't!"

"Yes you have! On my fun fourteenth you tried to get Peter's attention with all your camping skills."

"What are you talking about? It wasn't my fault that the canoe drifted," Zinnie protested.

"What is going on up here?" Aunt Sunny asked, joining them at the top of the stairs. She didn't look mad; she just looked worried and a little sad.

"Oh no," Zinnie said. "We're so sorry, Aunt Sunny."

"Sorry about what?" Aunt Sunny asked, wiping her hands on her apron.

"They promised they wouldn't fight in front of you," Lily said, peering out from behind Aunt Sunny. She had somehow sneaked up the stairs without anyone hearing. "And they almost made it." Lily shook her head, so very disappointed in them. "We were so close, guys!"

"Let's take a seat and have a talk," Aunt Sunny said, sitting on the little bed and gesturing for the sisters to join her. "What's the story?"

"Is everything okay up there?" Mom called from the floor below.

"We're just having a chat," Aunt Sunny said. "You go enjoy your swim, Gwen."

"I won't argue with that," Mom said.

They waited to hear the screen door shut behind her on her way out to the porch.

"Zinnie has sabotaged my relationship with Chloe!" Marigold said. "It all started when I was cast on the TV show. But I genuinely want to act, and Zinnie just needed something to write about, and she blogged about it anyway, so it doesn't even matter, does it?" Aunt Sunny didn't respond. She just listened. "And then, because I guess she needed to show everyone how great she is, she took all the attention away from me on my fun fourteenth!"

"It's not like I pushed the canoe in the river," Zinnie said.

"And this whole time, she's been trying to get Chloe to be her friend instead of mine," Marigold said, her voice cracking with emotion. "After this year, when I had so many friend issues. It's not nice. It's not . . . sisterly."

Aunt Sunny turned to Zinnie, who was surprisingly calm though also full of dread. She could feel the truth surfacing.

"Well, it's true that I was a little jealous of Marigold getting cast in the TV show," Zinnie said. "Sometimes it feels like she just always gets what she wants." It was harder than she thought it was going to be to say that aloud. "And it's also true that I really liked Chloe, so much that it felt like we were going to be best friends—if we had the time and if Marigold wasn't around."

"See, I told you!" Marigold said to Aunt Sunny as she wiped tears from her cheeks.

"Let her finish," Aunt Sunny said to Marigold, placing a hand on her arm. "So why did you disinvite Chloe tonight?"

"She's Brave13," Zinnie said.

Lily gasped. "She is?"

"What!" Marigold said, her eyes bulging. "How long have you known?"

"I didn't know until my last adventure—at the water tower. She met me there. She wanted to show me more places, too."

"This is unexpected," Aunt Sunny said. "I also thought it was Max, too shy to let on."

"Let on what?" Zinnie asked.

"That he fancies you," Aunt Sunny said.

Zinnie wanted to hear Aunt Sunny's take on this, but Marigold jumped in.

"This makes no sense!" Marigold said. "It's like she wanted to hang out with you, but without me." Zinnie held Marigold's gaze and let this sink in. "Wait. Am I right? Did she not want to be my friend?" Zinnie shook her head. "It's like Pilar all over again," Marigold said, bursting into tears.

"Oh, my dear," Aunt Sunny said, taking Marigold's hand. "This must really hurt."

"It does," Marigold said. "Why doesn't anyone want to be my friend?"

"Don't you see?" Zinnie said, becoming teary herself. "I want to be your friend. I'm going to miss you so much next year."

"What are you talking about?" Marigold asked. "We live together."

"But you're going to be at a new school. All the way across town. I've never gone to school without you, and I don't want to. And it hurt my feelings so much that you didn't want me to hang around you this summer. As soon as you met Chloe, you were ready to ditch me," Zinnie said, drying her eyes with the edge of her T-shirt.

"I'm sorry," Marigold said. "I'm really, really sorry. You're the best friend I could have."

"What about me?" Lily asked.

"You too," Marigold said. And the three sisters hugged.

"Now tell me again why you made this promise not to fight," Aunt Sunny said, wrapping her arms around all three of them.

"We didn't want to upset you like we did last year," Zinnie said. "When we almost ruined your wedding."

"I appreciate your thoughtfulness, but you must

remember that I had sisters, too. And the best thing about having them is that you can fight, you can express your feelings—including your hurts, your anger, and your fears—because you know in your hearts that they'll always be there for you," Aunt Sunny said. "And anyway. It's not good to keep your feelings pushed down inside you. It's not healthy for a body! And they're going to find their way up somehow, believe me! Better to get them out in the open as soon as possible. And you can't just pretend you don't have certain feelings. It doesn't work. You're much better off acknowledging your emotions. They're nothing to be ashamed of."

"They aren't?" Zinnie asked. Aunt Sunny looked her deep in the eyes and shook her head. "Does this just apply to sisters?" Zinnie hated avoiding Max—but it was the only way to hide her true feelings for him.

"Of course not," Aunt Sunny said. "Now, you can't control how other people respond to you, but as long as you're not hurting anyone, it's healthy to express yourself. It's my experience that you only injure yourself by hiding your truth. In fact, it takes so much energy to deny your emotions that doing so can eat you up inside."

"It *is* eating me up inside!" Zinnie declared, throwing her hands into the air and collapsing back onto the bed.

"What is?" Lily asked.

"My feelings for Max," Zinnie said. "I like him so much that I'm tangled up and I can't get out of my head, I can't even remember simple song lyrics or do basic improvisations. I'm not myself!"

Marigold laughed, but not in a mean way.

"What?" Zinnie asked, her shoulders shaking. Releasing her emotions had given her the giggles. Then Lily started laughing, too.

"My dear," Aunt Sunny said, kissing the top of Zinnie's head. "Don't you see? In telling me all this, you are being you. Your true self is only a few questions away—always. 'Is this me?' you can ask yourself. 'Is this really me?' You can feel in your heart when you get to the truth—and that's a mighty good feeling."

"Can I put that in my blog?" Zinnie asked, recognizing good words when she heard them.

"Of course," Aunt Sunny said. "I don't know if it'll get you in Huzzah, but it might help you have a little fun tonight."

Zinnie laughed. She hadn't realized that Aunt Sunny had been following all of this—but she wouldn't be Aunt Sunny if she hadn't been. Anyway, right now, getting into Huzzah didn't feel very important.

And as usual, Aunt Sunny was right.

For the rest of the evening, Zinnie stopped trying to hide her emotions from Max. In fact, before dinner was ready, she asked him if he wanted to have a swimming contest and he said, "Heck, yeah," and they jumped off opposite sides of the ladder and raced back to the steps. He won, but Zinnie didn't care. She just floated on her back and grinned at the sky.

43 · The Tricentennial

Marigold awoke with great anticipation the next morning.

The day of celebration had finally arrived, and she was ready for it. After their discussion with Aunt Sunny last night, Zinnie had relaxed. The sisters and Max rehearsed their song several times for the adults, and with each practice it had improved. Zinnie had been right—they didn't need any help from Chloe.

The thought of Chloe stung Marigold. Another "cool" girl had rejected her. She let herself feel sad for a minute, and yet, she couldn't get *too* sad about it. She didn't really know Chloe that well, and if she was anything like the Cuties . . . Well, she'd had enough of that. She asked herself, *Is this me?* as Aunt Sunny had suggested. But she'd only had to ask herself once. The answer was yes.

The Silver family, Aunt Sunny, and Tony rose early to meet Jean, Mack, Peter, and Max and his parents at the yacht club, which was decorated to perfection. Together, they walked up to Charlotte Point, where it felt like the whole town had gathered. Marigold's palms tingled as the crowd chatted, making guesses about who the town council would name James and Eliza Pruet. Two fine-looking horses were all saddled up, ready to lead the parade.

She glanced around, wondering who her competition might be. Ashley? Vince? One of those kids from the high school in their Pruet High sweatshirts? Her mouth was dry. She guzzled her bottle of water. Finally, the town council members took their places in front of the group. Ashley's father, who was the head of the council, raised a hand to silence the crowd.

"Welcome, everyone, to the Pruet tricentennial parade!" he said. The crowd cheered. "We have so many fun activities for you today. I know we can't wait to get started. Our first order of business is to name James and Eliza Pruet."

Marigold took a deep breath and grabbed her mother's hand.

"Would Jean and Mack Pasque please step forward," Ashley's dad said with a grin. Marigold felt a cold drop of disappointment land in her stomach, but it didn't stay there long. Jean was blushing and grinning like crazy. She looked like a teenager! Aunt Sunny whooped and Tony clapped louder than anyone.

"What!" Jean said as she and Mack approached the town council members. Jean was holding the crown of flowers in her hand—after all, she'd made it herself.

"You can go ahead and place that on your head, Jean," Ashley's dad said. "There's no one here who has done more for this community than the two of you— especially after the storm."

"Well, okay," Jean said, turning a deeper shade of crimson as she placed the crown of flowers on her head and mounted the horse. "If you insist."

Peter was also red in the face! *So Peter got his blushing capacity from his mom,* Marigold thought, and giggled.

"I thought this was for young folks," Mack said as he climbed on his horse. He reached over and kissed his wife's hand.

"Why, you look just like a couple of kids in love," Aunt Sunny said. And lots of people laughed. They did! Peter had now buried his face in his sweatshirt.

Marigold was over the loss already. Jean and Mack clearly deserved the recognition more than Marigold, and she followed happily behind them.

The parade began at Charlotte Point, with the high school marching band behind Mack and Jean. Peter and his friends all wore sailing team T-shirts and waved flags with the symbol of the Pruet Yacht Club. Edith, wearing an Edith's Ice Cream apron, proudly walked Mocha Chip along with everyone else. The Silver family walked together, somewhere in the middle.

Once everyone arrived at the town beach, Ashley blew a foghorn and then announced through a megaphone that the sand castle building competition was underway. "Grab your buckets and shovels," she said. "You have exactly thirty minutes to build your sand castles!"

"Let's do this," Dad said, and the Silver family huddled and agreed they would build the best replica of Aunt Sunny's home that they could. Aunt Sunny and Tony helped, but after a few minutes their castle wasn't looking so great, so they turned it into a mermaid with wild seaweed hair and smile made of shells. Then they buried Dad up to his chin and made him a merman. Lily laughed as she fashioned a long and smelly seaweed beard for him. They didn't win, but nobody really had a chance against Ashley's dad, who turned out to be a master sand sculptor, in addition to owning the second-most successful car dealership on Cape Cod.

Marigold didn't think she'd ever be able to get all the sand off her in time for their song—the sand had found its way in between her toes and under her fingernails and even in her hair—but she didn't have time to go back to Aunt Sunny's and take a shower, at least not if she wanted the performance to be set up properly. Next on the itinerary was the historical houses tour, ending at the Piping Plover Society, where Aunt Sunny had set up several exhibits with information about the local wildlife. And after that was the regatta—which she wouldn't miss for the world. So she decided that it just didn't matter if there was sand in the cuffs of her shorts as long her hands were scrubbed clean.

She looked around for Peter—she wanted to wish him good luck—but she didn't see him in the crowd or as she, Zinnie, and Lily walked to the yacht club to prepare.

The girls set up their tables and the ice cream truck facade while their parents hung the ice cream banners and Edith rolled out the mobile freezers full of ice cream ready to be served. In the distance Marigold saw the sailing teams getting ready. She sent her wishes to him on the breeze. After the bulk of the work was done and all that was left was setting up the toppings bar, Max arrived with his guitar in hand.

"Why don't you two start practicing while Lily and I get everything else in order?" Marigold said.

"Okey-dokey, artichokey!" Zinnie said, and Marigold watched her sister's face fill with color. "I mean, sure. That's cool."

Max just laughed in his good-natured way and tuned his guitar.

Zinnie and Max began practicing, but Zinnie was acting stiff and nervous.

Marigold pulled Zinnie aside, out of earshot of Max. "Look, I think he likes you, too. And remember what Aunt Sunny said—don't try to hide your feelings. It's not healthy."

"But I like him so much that half the time I feel like I'm going to throw up!" Zinnie said. "That doesn't seem healthy, either."

"Try to relax and have a good time," Marigold said. "You did last night."

"But it's started all over again this morning!"

"Then don't fight it. Just be nervous. Be who you are," Marigold said, but Zinnie was looking paler by the second. "What are you so nervous about?"

"I don't even know," Zinnie said. "My knees are shaking; my armpits are sweating! Do I smell okay?"

"You smell fine," Marigold said. "Look, no matter what happens with Max, we'll deal with it. Or you can write a blog post about it."

"I guess having a crush is a kind of adventure," Zinnie said.

"It might be the greatest adventure of all," Marigold said. "Isn't that what most songs and movies are about?"

"Everything okay over there?" Max asked.

"Yup," Marigold called back. Then she took Zinnie's hands and said, "Isn't it a nice feeling to like someone so much?"

Zinnie nodded. "It is. It really is. I like him so much. I feel like I'm made of bubbles."

"Go with that," Marigold said. "Be bubbles!"

As Zinnie bravely walked back toward Max, Marigold decided that sending Peter a wish on the breeze wasn't good enough. This was his big moment, and she wanted to be there for him.

"I'll be right back, okay?" she called to Zinnie, who gave her a thumbs-up.

Marigold walked down to the docks, where the sailors were readying their boats.

"Marigold," Peter said with a smile when he spotted her, and the sound of her name in his voice made her pulse jump. "Are you getting ready for the ice cream social and your performance?"

"Yes," Marigold said. "But I just wanted to say good luck to you guys."

"Thanks," Peter said. Vince waved at her. "One minute, Vince."

"No problem," Vince said, turning his attention back to their sailboat.

"Come here for a second," Peter said, taking her hand and leading her to end of the dock. They sat down and let their feet dangle over the edge.

"Don't you have to get ready?" Marigold asked.

"Vince has everything under control," Peter said.

"You seem so relaxed. I thought you'd be

supernervous," Marigold said.

"I like to head into a competition happy," Peter said. "I've noticed that's when I do my best. So I try not to let my nerves get the best of me."

"I'm like that with auditions," Marigold said.

"There's something I think that would make me really happy right now," Peter said.

"What's that?" Marigold asked, though she had a feeling she knew what it was. There were goose bumps on her arms and legs even though the bright July sun warmed her skin.

Peter smiled at her, leaned over, and gave her a sweet, quick kiss on the lips.

44 · Family Portrait

Zinnie stepped onto the stage and saw Max waiting for her. For a moment her hands started to shake and her knees went wobbly. *Be a bubble,* she thought. *Be a bubble.* And she floated toward him, light and airy with a bounce in her step. Oh my goodness, did he smile big—as big as ever!

"And now," Zinnie said to the crowd. "The Silver sisters and Max present 'Why We Love Pruet.'"

The sisters took turns performing, and by the end, the entire audience was singing the chorus. Zinnie looked over at Max and beamed right back at her.

"Let's hear it for the Silver sisters," Jean said, clapping. The audience hooted and hollered. Aunt Sunny stood up, and their dad gave a taxicab whistle.

That night the clambake on the lawn was spectacular. Unlike the little clambake they'd had at the beach a few summers ago, there was a huge pile of seaweed and lots of people tending to it.

"Come here," Zinnie said to Max. "I want to show you something really cool." She told her sisters she'd be back in a moment, and then she took Max to the water tower. They climbed up the sides.

"I like you," Zinnie said. "Ugh, there I said it. I like you."

"I like you, too," Max said.

"You do?" Zinnie asked.

"Yes!" Max said.

Zinnie was about to ask him what his mystery was all about when he added, "In fact, I was going to ask you to be my first kiss."

"What?" Zinnie said, though it was more of an exclamation than a question.

He stepped a little closer to her. "Do you want to?"

"Yes," Zinnie said. "But I've never kissed anyone before either. I mean, not like that."

"Good," Max said. "Then we're in this together. Let's not do it like they do in the movies."

"Yeah, that looks crazy," Zinnie agreed. "When they lean all over each other. And tilt their heads. Do you *have* to tilt your head, though?"

"Let's just stop talking about it and try, okay?" Max said.

"Okay," Zinnie said. "I'm going to close my eyes now."

"Me too," Max said. They knocked heads and both burst out laughing.

"Maybe one of us should open our eyes," Zinnie said.

"Or both of us should open one eye," Max suggested.

"That's too weird," Zinnie said. "You look like a Cyclops." Max blushed, and Zinnie corrected herself. "The cutest Cyclops in the whole world."

Then before she had time to think, Max took ahold of her shoulders and planted a sweet, light kiss right on her lips.

"Yay," Zinnie said softly.

"Yay," said Max. And then they did it again.

After they watched the sunset from atop the water tower, Zinnie and Max hopped onto their bikes and headed back to the yacht club, through the country roads, and around the curve where cars traveled quickly. A breeze cooled her face as they rode past Featherbrook Farm. A few chickens pecked at some feed near the sign, and Zinnie waved at them.

She and Max didn't speak as they pedaled. Instead, they just cruised as the bugs made their night noises and the wheels of their bikes created quiet shushing sounds. Zinnie thought to herself that she had never felt so free. Even if Chloe had caused some issues with

Marigold, even though keeping another secret from Marigold had been a bump in the smooth road of summer, Zinnie was still glad that she'd met her. It had been Chloe who'd directed her to all these cool places and who'd encouraged her to leave her comfort zone. Zinnie didn't see Chloe as a friend going forward. It would be way too weird to hang out with her when she was going to school with Marigold. But she was still grateful to have met her. Maybe, Zinnie thought as they rode toward town, exploring so many new places in the outside world had given her the courage to take some internal risks as well. Even if Chloe's clues hadn't led to her getting published in Huzzah, they'd somehow led her to this moment with Max.

They turned down Harbor Road, which was blocked off from traffic because of the tricentennial, and Max stood on his bike as he coasted downhill. He turned around for a moment and smiled at Zinnie. Her heart spun like a pinwheel in the breeze.

When they got to the yacht club they leaned their bikes in the grass and walked toward the clambake, which was winding down. Zinnie could hear Edith all the way from the driveway. She was describing some new flavors for the fall: apple pie ice cream with bits of pie crust inside; nutmeg butternut squash; and pumpkin pie filling, swirled with marshmallow fluff, cinnamon, and toasted coconut.

"Zinnie, there you are," Lily said. "Come here. We're

going to take a family picture for our holiday card."

"Oh, okay," Zinnie said. "But we didn't plan what we're going to wear or anything." Usually, Mom wanted them to be in coordinated outfits for their holiday card, and almost always, they took the holiday photo at the pumpkin patch near their house, the one set up by the local rotary club, with the bouncy house and the scarecrow.

"I know, but it's happening anyway, and everyone is looking for you," Lily said.

"I'll be right there," Zinnie said. She wanted one more moment alone with Max. She smiled at him, and he smiled back. "Where are you going to be living next year?"

"That's my big surprise," Max said. "My dad is going to be stationed at the base in Monterey."

"In California?" Zinnie asked, nearly beside herself with joy. Monterey wasn't exactly next door, but it was in the same state! Max nodded. Zinnie kissed him on the cheek. She didn't even care who saw. Then she ran over to her family.

"Zinnie," Dad said when she ran up to hug him. "Where'd you go?"

"I wanted to show Max the water tower," Zinnie said.

"Really?" Dad asked, looking a little pale.

"I think I might be in love," Zinnie said.

Mom and Dad exchanged a glance.

"'Might be'?" Marigold said. "Please, this girl is head over heels!"

"You are?" Lily asked, looking horrified.

"That's wonderful," Dad said, though Zinnie saw his eyes filling up.

"Dad, are you crying?" Zinnie asked.

Dad shook his head, but he used the heel of his hands to wipe away tears.

"And we're so glad that you felt you could tell us," Mom said, nudging Dad. "We hope you'll always feel good about telling us your feelings."

"Now listen, if you have any questions at all—" Dad started.

"Stop!" Zinnie was regretting this. "Haven't we already had this discussion?"

"I'm really happy for you," Dad said. "I can't believe how grown-up you are."

"Are you ready?" Aunt Sunny asked, holding up her camera.

"Are you crazy, Aunt Sunny?" Mom asked. "Don't you know we want you in this?"

"Okay," Aunt Sunny said. She handed the camera to Tony.

"Tony, you need to come here as well," Dad said. Tony smiled and passed the camera to Max.

"Shouldn't Max be in the picture, because he's Tony's grandson?" Lily said.

Max laughed and passed the camera on to Jean.

"Jean is like family," Aunt Sunny said.

Jean started laughing. "I think we can see where this is headed!"

Jean, Mack, and Peter joined in the picture, and then Edith and Mocha Chip came in as well, and before they knew it, Ashley was walking by, and she had to be in the picture, too. It was none other than the famous director Mr. Rathbone himself who took the photo.

"That's a lot of people for our holiday card," Lily said.

"We'll do another one later," Mom said, and gave Lily a squeeze.

After many pictures were snapped with everyone's phones, and they were all headed over to the beach for the fireworks display, Marigold pulled Zinnie aside. Lily was close behind.

"You kissed him," she said. Zinnie bit her lip and looked away. "I knew it!"

"How did you know?" Lily asked.

"It's written all over Zinnie's face," Marigold said. "You might as well be wearing a neon sign."

"Really?" Zinnie asked. Marigold nodded. Zinnie pressed her fingers to her cheeks. They were burning up.

"Are you going to write about it in your blog?" Marigold asked.

"Nope," Zinnie said, and linked her arms in her

sisters'. "I'm going to keep this to myself."

"Except that you told us!" Lily said.

"Yeah, but you're my sisters," Zinnie said.

"So?" Lily asked.

"So she trusts us," Marigold said.

"Exactly," Zinnie said, and pulled them both a little closer to her. It was true. She did trust them, with her heart and her secrets. For a moment she could feel the earth under her feet, holding her up as though she had roots, and the sky above her, beckoning her to look up, up, up. She inhaled the summer air and felt so much a part of this family, a part of this world.

Acknowledgments

Thank you to my brilliant editor, Alexandra Cooper. Working on these books with you has been an incredible honor and joy. As always, I thank my agent and friend, Sara Crowe, for everything. And many thanks, as well, to the amazing Alyssa Miele, who is endlessly helpful and full of great ideas. Thank you to Ji-Hyuk Kim for the gorgeous artwork, and to everyone at HarperCollins who helped make this dream come true. I am truly indebted to fellow writers Kayla Cagan and Vanessa Napolitano, my LA sisters and friends to the end. Thank you to my family, especially Henry, who I'm pretty certain hung the moon.

EXPLORE THE SUMMER MAGIC OF CAPE COD WITH THE SILVER SISTERS!